I0662573

Grove

of

Ghosts

Grove of Ghosts

by

Laura Stachel

Copyright notice

Laura Stachel, 2025

All right reserved. No part of this book may be reproduced, stored in a retrieval system, or transmitted in any form or by any means, electronic, photocopying, mechanical' recording or otherwise, without the prior permission of the copyright author.

for Buddy, who opened my heart,
and Hula, who showed me the way to use it…

TABLE OF CONTENTS

~ Prologue ~

In the summer of 1586, Queen Elizabeth I, driven by national ambition and the promise of wealth, intensified her interest in establishing an English presence in the New World. Inspired by reports from earlier explorers who described the lands across the Atlantic as fertile and abundant, she granted a charter to Sir Walter Raleigh. The patent authorized him to claim and settle any unoccupied territories in the name of the Crown. The newly envisioned colony was named "Virginia," in honor of Elizabeth, the "Virgin Queen."

The following year, Raleigh organized an expedition of 117 men, women, and children to create a more permanent settlement on Roanoke Island, off the coast of present-day North Carolina. He appointed John White as governor of the new colony, which was to be called the "Cittie of Raleigh." Among the colonists were White's pregnant daughter, Eleanor Dare; her husband, Ananias Dare; and Manteo, a Croatoan chief who had traveled to England and become an ally to the English.

In July 1587, the settlers disembarked on Roanoke Island. Almost immediately, they were met with troubling news: fifteen men from a previous expedition had been killed by local Indigenous groups. Unease spread among the colonists, yet they moved forward with their plans to establish a foothold in the New World. On August 18, 1587, Eleanor Dare gave birth to a daughter, Virginia—marking the first recorded birth of an English child on American soil.

Just ten days later, Governor White reluctantly returned to England to seek additional supplies and reinforcements for the struggling colony. It would prove to be a fateful decision. Upon arriving in England, White's return voyage was delayed by the looming threat of invasion by the Spanish Armada. Naval resources were redirected toward national defense, and White was unable to secure passage back to Roanoke for nearly three years.

Finally, on August 18, 1590—his granddaughter's third birthday—White returned to Roanoke Island. What he found shocked him. The settlement had been abandoned and showed signs of being plundered. Surrounding the site was a palisade of tall trees arranged in a fort-like structure. Carved into one of the posts was the word "CROATOAN"; nearby, the letters "CRO" were etched into a tree.

Before leaving for England in 1587, White had agreed upon a system of communication with the colonists: if they were forced to relocate, they would inscribe the name of their destination; if they left under threat, they would also add a Maltese cross. No such cross was found, suggesting the move had been voluntary. White hoped the message indicated the settlers had relocated to Croatoan Island (modern-day Hatteras Island), home to Chief Manteo's people.

Despite his hopes, White was never able to organize a follow-up expedition to search for the colonists. The fate of the 117 settlers—men, women, and children—remains one of the most enduring mysteries in American history. The disappearance of the Roanoke colony would come to be known as "The Lost Colony," a haunting symbol of the risks and uncertainties of early colonial ventures.

~ 1 ~

Journal of Eleanor Dare
1587 - 1588

The 6th Day of Februare, in the Year of our Lord 1587
This day, my Father, Master John White, did come unto
me with most wondrous and joyful news: Her Majesty the
Queen hath named him Governour of the first English
Colonie to be planted in the New World. The charge is
great, and the honour greater still. Preparations are
already in motion, and we are to set forth within a
fortnight. My heart is full of marvel and anticipation—for
what greater adventure might there be than to cross the
vast Ocean Sea and begin a new life upon a land
unknown?

The 22th Day of Julie, 1587
At long last we have made landfall, our ships anchoring
near the place called Roanoak. The voyage was long and
sore, the latter days most grievous unto me, for I was
heavy with child and longed to stand again upon God's
earth. Yet the land is wild and most harsh, with thick
woods and marshes, and the sun bites cruelly.

Straightaway we began to unship our victuals and
goods, setting to work to fetch water and timber. We had

hoped to find fifteene men left from a former voyage, yet found naught but bones. 'Twas a grim welcome.

Manteo, a native man of the Croatoan, who hath journeyed with us from England, speaks our tongue and doth act as peacemaker. There was blood spilt by our countrymen aforetime, who slew the chief of the Secotan people. Thus our arrival is shadowed by mistrust. With Manteo's aid, we hope to amend what hath been done and seek friendship with those who know this land.

The 18th Day of August, 1587
This day hath brought forth joy unmatched: I, Eleanor Dare, daughter of the Governour and wife to Master Ananias Dare, was delivered of a daughter, here upon the soil of Virginia. The child was christened upon the Sunday following, and given the name Virginia, for she is the first Christian child borne unto English parents in this new land. I thank God for her safe coming.

The 22th Day of August, 1587
Today the whole of our company—both the Assistants and the planters—did gather before my Father and did entreat him earnestly to return to England, there to procure succour for us. Our provisions run thin, and we came too late in the season to plant any crop. Without aid, many fear we shall not see the spring.

My Father's heart was heavy. He loves his granddaughter, little Virginia, and he did not wish to part from us so soon. Yet the voices of the people were many and urgent, and in the end, he did consent. As Governour, he could not turn away from his duty.

He made plan that we should remove our settlement fifty miles into the maine, to a more secure place where our goods may be kept safe from weather and theft. There we are to dwell until his return.

Though my heart is sore at his departure, I do keep faith that he shall return swiftly, and with all the aid we so dearly need.

The 27th Day of August, 1587

This day, my Father and nine others took sail back unto England. Before his departure, we did agree upon a pact: should we need to leave our dwelling, we would carve into a tree the name of the place whither we had gone, so that he might find us upon his return. If we must depart hastily, a cross would be carved beside the name as a dire warning.

The 8th Day of September, 1587

Throughout this autumn, we have moved our fort unto the Cittie of Raleigh, as was decided with my Father. The Croatoan have been most helpful and kind. They have come unto us bearing food, and have welcomed us into their camps, teaching us their gentle ways. They showed us how to catch and prepare the local game, how to carve trees into canoes, and how to fish from them. They also gave us seeds to plant and taught us to work the soil.

They are greatly taken with little Virginia, the first white child born upon this soil. They teach her their tongue, and we teach her English in return. Her blue eyes do marvel them, for such a colour they have never before beheld. We do hope each day that my Father shall return with supplies, and our hearts are full of hope that we shall survive the coming winter.

The 25th Day of September, 1587

Manteo did remind me today of the dreadful tale of the former settlers. Several years ago, another company of English did attempt to settle here. A silver cup was stolen by an Indian, and in anger, the English captured the chief of the Secotan, named Wingina, and did burn him alive before his village. They then set fire to the crops when the cup was not returned.

This cruel act set the Secotan against us, and Manteo was quick to warn me of this. Knowing my station as the Governour's daughter, I did take care to treat the Secotan always with respect and kindness, hoping thereby to lead the others to do the same.

The 15th Day of October, 1587

On many occasions when we went to harvest our crops, we found them burning. The Secotan do make it their purpose to frighten us away or to starve us out. Yet, whenever they sought to destroy us, the Croatoan stood beside us to aid and defend. Without their help, we surely would have perished.

Winter, 1588
Winter hath come harsh and cruel. The snows fell heavy, and the food hath been scarce. We would have all starved were it not for the generosity of the Croatoan, who saved us many times over.

We have lost five children to the fever, and four women are with child, two of whom are in great peril this cruel season. I fear they may not see the spring.

A strange beast hath wandered near the Citie. It is larger than a horse, with four legs, a great head covered in white woolly hair, and two horns upon its brow. The colonists believed it a gift from God to aid us in winter's grasp.

Manteo warned me not to harm this white "buffalo," for it is sacred and carries great magic. To harm it would bring destruction upon the land and its people.

The colonists did mock this warning and slew the buffalo to feed themselves. Yet, no fire would light, no matter how much wood they laid to the flames. The salt they had for curing meat vanished. Those who ate of the buffalo grew sick and pleaded for the Croatoan's healing, but help was denied.

Within three days, nearly half the colonists, forty-four souls, were dead, leaving only fifty-nine alive. A week hence, the buffalo disappeared. When morning came, it was gone without trace.

Spring, 1588
At last, spring hath returned, and with it, new life. A child was born to Sara Payne and a Croatoan man named Tacumwah, wed this past summer. They named their son Orotam. Virginia and Orotam, close in age, spend many hours together.

My Father hath not returned as soon as we hoped. Though the winter was hard, we survived with the help of our Croatoan friends. Yet we mourn the loss of forty-nine souls, from sickness and hunger. We began with one hundred fifteen men, women, and children; now but sixty remain, counting Virginia and Orotam.

Summer, 1588
We have been blessed with two more babes, born of Indian and English parentage. We now have four Croatoan children with the rare blue-grey eyes living among us.

My Father's return remains uncertain. Many fear he hath perished upon the sea. Yet we cling to hope he will come back with supplies and new settlers.

Meanwhile, the Croatoan continue to teach us how and when to plant. With their help, we might endure the next winter.

The 18th Day of September, 1588

Knowing the coming winter shall be harsh once more, we resolved to leave the Cittie of Raleigh and dwell with the Croatoan. We took down our homes and moved our supplies to their encampment, carving the word "CROATOAN" upon a nearby palisade — the signal my Father and we had agreed upon before his departure.

The 23th Day of September, 1588

Today we closed the fort and dismantled the houses and fortifications. All our belongings were packed, and we journeyed toward the Croatoan camp.

But fifteen miles from Raleigh, we were set upon by a rival Indian faction, the Secotan. They came suddenly, with bows and hatchets. Each of us seized our children and fled through the woods, leaving all behind, fleeing the screams and fury of the attack…

~ 2 ~

Beechland

February, 2029

The funeral was stilted and uncomfortable, a strange blend of formality and raw emotion. The first three pews of the church were marked "Family Only," yet Jenny sat alone in the front row, a solitary figure in a place meant for many. Behind her, the pews were packed—friends, neighbors, former colleagues—all gathered to honor her late uncle, Brian Ritter. She could feel their glances, not unkind but heavy with sympathy, wrapping around her like an unwelcome quilt of sympathy.

She kept her eyes fixed on her lap, where her hands twisted in anxious, relentless motion. Her knuckles blanched as she gripped her fingers tightly, trying to hold herself together.

The church buzzed softly with whispered greetings and the rustling of coats. Jenny scanned the faces behind her but recognized no one. She had been gone too long—first emotionally, then physically. Time had eroded the familiar.

Just as the organ began to hum the first notes of the prelude, a figure slid into the seat beside her. George Strumbel.

His presence brought an unexpected wave of comfort. He was her uncle's longtime friend and estate planner, a fixture in Brian's life for over four decades since their college roommate days. His smile was warm, seasoned with sorrow and understanding.

George was a short, bald, round man with a thick white mustache that curled slightly at the ends, like it had been borrowed from a storybook or a board game. Jenny had always thought he looked like the Monopoly man—surely there was a top hat and cane hidden somewhere in his house.

The service began, and voices rose with reverence and memory. Friends shared heartfelt stories of Brian's quiet generosity, his mentorship, his fierce loyalty. He had been a cornerstone of many lives—firm, humble, and deeply kind. Though the grief in the room was palpable, it mingled with deep gratitude. Brian Ritter had not just lived a good life; he had lived one that mattered.

After the final hymn faded and the congregation filed out, Jenny stepped into the crisp afternoon light outside the church. George found her near her car, his coat buttoned tight against the cold.

He offered her a hug, then pressed an envelope into her hands.

"Your Uncle Brian loved you very much, Jenny," he said, his voice gentle. "His illness came on fast, but he made sure to set a few things in motion before the end. This... this is for you."

George handed her an envelope. Inside it was a single key. Written on the front in Brian's familiar, was an address:

7588 Manteo Lane
Beechland, VA

George calmed Jenny's curiosity with a kind smile and a quiet promise: "All will be explained in time."

After the funeral, Jenny didn't linger. The city had too many memories, and every familiar street corner reminded her of a life she was trying to leave behind. She packed a few bags, slipped quietly out of Boston, and headed south toward Beechland. Eleven hours of open road stretched in front of her, and for once, she welcomed the silence. She didn't turn on the radio. The hum of the engine and the rhythm of the tires on pavement were enough. She needed time to think. To grieve. To begin again.

The trip wasn't just about distance. It was about space— emotional space to process everything that had unraveled over the last two years. Her marriage. Her pregnancies. The way love had soured into silence, then into something far crueler.

She had met Nicholas Darrington Jr. at the West Dover Polo Club, near Boston. She was working in the barns, cleaning out stalls, a job she loved despite the dirt. Nicholas had been hanging out with his usual group of elite friends when he wandered past a stall just as Jenny tossed a heavy shovel full of manure. He stepped right into the line of fire.

It hit him square in the chest.

Jenny had gasped. "Holy crap! I'm so sorry!" His friends stared at her like she was a stray dog who'd wandered into their dining room, but Nicholas just laughed.

"It's okay," he said, brushing himself off. "I should've known better than to walk past a stall without checking first." And then, he looked at her. Really looked. There was something in his eyes—not pity, not amusement. Curiosity.

His friends didn't share the sentiment. They looked at Jenny like she was dirt under their designer boots. Still, he introduced himself. Not just "Nick" or "Nicky," but Nicholas Darrington Jr. He even kissed her hand, like something out of an old movie. Jenny had been terrified. She didn't belong in his world, and everyone there knew it. Everyone except him.

Their romance bloomed quickly, dangerously. It was passionate and messy and intoxicating. Nicholas called her "Hun," a nickname he said came from her dark hair and high cheekbones. "You remind me of the Huns," he once said with a boyish grin. "Fierce. Beautiful. Unstoppable." She had laughed it off at the time, but secretly, it touched her.

They married a year later in a lavish ceremony that felt more like a Darrington family affair than a celebration of love. Jenny wore a designer gown loaned by Nicholas's mother and smiled through a reception filled with people she didn't know. His family never outright rejected her—but they never welcomed her either. She was a novelty, a curiosity, a phase they hoped he would grow out of.

And then came the pregnancies. The first one brought joy, if only briefly. Jenny miscarried at eight weeks. Nicholas said all the right things, but there was a distance in his eyes. A resignation. His parents were coldly practical. "These things happen," his mother had said. "Just try again."

Uncle Brian had been the only one who truly mourned with her. "It's OK, Jenny," he said, sitting beside her on the couch, gently holding her hand. "You'll get through this. I promise. Everything will be OK."

The second pregnancy ended at twelve weeks. Jenny had done everything right—no riding, no stress, strict bed rest for weeks. Still, it wasn't enough. And this time, Nicholas wasn't as kind. He didn't say it outright, but Jenny could feel it: he blamed her. As though her body had failed him.

That was when he told her. His inheritance was conditional—hinged on producing a male heir to carry on the Darrington name. His sisters couldn't do it. As the only male child, only he could. And Jenny, in his eyes, was standing in the way.

Their third pregnancy was the most difficult. The doctors ordered complete bed rest. Nicholas hired a nurse—really more of a maid—and Jenny was confined to the bedroom for weeks on end. No visitors. No movement. No life. It was isolating, claustrophobic, and terrifying. She waited every day for Nicholas to visit, to check on her. But he came less and less. Always busy. Always gone.

When she miscarried for the third time, the nurse was the one who held her while she cried. Nicholas wasn't even home.

One month later, she was served divorce papers. Neat. Cold. Final. Nicholas had been seeing someone else. She was pregnant. His heir was on the way.

Jenny didn't scream. She didn't beg. She packed her things and drove straight to Uncle Brian's cabin. There, at least, she was loved. Safe.

She collapsed into his arms, her pain spilling out in broken sobs and breathless sentences. He listened. He didn't interrupt. He made her tea and wrapped her in a blanket like he had when she was a child. "It's OK, Jenny," he whispered. "You don't have to fight anymore. Everything will be OK."

He kept his promise. Three months later, he was gone.

Now, she was driving to Beechland, with the key he had left behind. She didn't know what waited for her, but it was the only thing that felt like hope. The past had taken so much. Her future was still unwritten.

And this—whatever this was—felt like the first page of something new.

~ ~ * ~ ~

This road trip couldn't have come at a better time. Jenny told herself it was just a quick detour—one night in a hotel, a call to a local real estate agent in the morning, and then she'd be done. She didn't need the house, and she certainly didn't need the money. The prenup with Nicholas had been airtight: no heir, no inheritance. But then came the betrayal—and the baby. Not hers.

Nicholas's affair hadn't just ended their marriage. It had rewritten every moment they'd shared, every promise he'd ever made. To make it go away quietly and without legal drama, his

18

family offered Jenny a sizable settlement. Hush money. It was meant to erase the past, to make it easier for her to disappear. And for a while, she had. But this drive, this mystery house gifted to her by Uncle Brian—it felt like the first move toward something more than just disappearing.

Her grip on the steering wheel of her little Mazda Miata tightened the more she thought about Nicholas—how foolishly she'd believed they could build a life together. Her hands ached by the time the pain crawled up to her elbows, and she forced herself to relax, stretching her fingers wide, one by one.

She reached the turnoff just past a line of endless white fencing. It followed the road like a ribbon, curling with the hills before disappearing into trees. A small, unassuming dirt road cut to the left—no sign, no gate. Just the number etched into a simple wooden post.

The path wove through a shaded grove, the canopy of branches dappling the sunlight across her windshield. And then, as suddenly as the trees had begun, they gave way to a wide clearing—and the property.

Three buildings stood before her like something out of a painting: a barn, a shed, and a house. The barn and shed were neat, new, and functional. The house, however, carried the weight of time in its bones.

She pulled up in front of the house and stepped out, stretching her spine as she took it in. It was an old farmhouse, definitely at least century old, with the kind of charm no new construction could fake—yet it had been restored with clear care. The windows were new. The roof looked fresh. Uncle

Brian's touch was everywhere, and she suspected his construction company had taken on the project personally.

She walked first toward the barn. The scent of raw lumber and paint still lingered, and the air was warm inside despite the wide-open space. It was a classic red barn with crisp white trim and a gambrel roof that curved proudly overhead. Six stalls lined the interior—four 12'x12' regular-sized on the left, and two foaling stalls, 14'x16' on the right. The place had clearly never housed horses; it was pristine, untouched. It felt like a promise waiting to be fulfilled.

She explored the tack room—dozens of hooks, a place for everything. The back room had a stainless-steel fridge, cabinets, even a first-aid corner that smelled faintly of antiseptic. In the loft, the wide hatch in the floor could drop hay easily to the stalls below. Thoughtful. Practical. Uncle Brian all over again.

But the heat was building. Jenny wandered to the house next, pulling the key from the envelope and fitting it into the lock. The moment she stepped through the door, she was met the sight of a grand staircase rising from the foyer. Above it hung a chandelier—elegant but understated, just right for the space.

To the left, a generous living room, all wide windows and soft light. To the right, a small dining room that led into a kitchen gleaming with new stainless-steel appliances. There was a sliding glass door between the kitchen and the living room at the back of the house. When both doors were open, the breeze throughout the house kept it cool.

Every corner of the house had been touched—new paint, polished floors, even fresh curtains swaying in the breeze from open windows. Someone had poured heart and soul into making it not just livable, but *welcoming*.

The furnishings were surprisingly perfect—soft, neutral tones, classic lines. Not flashy, just comforting. The kind of place that made you want to curl up with a blanket and a book.

She wandered up the stairs. The hallway branched left and right. To the left, two modest bedrooms with a shared bath. The rooms themselves were simple. But the bathroom doorframe stopped her cold. Its chipped, aging paint had been left untouched. On one side, a series of notches were carved into the wood—tiny marks labeled "PJ" and "Ginny." The names sparked something faint, something deep in her bones. A memory. Two children, laughing, chasing each other, whispering secret nicknames.

The names were gone from the present but etched into the past.

She stepped into the master bedroom and found it breathtaking. Vaulted ceilings. A panoramic view of the pasture. A skylight overhead. The bathroom was spa-like, complete with a soaking tub, natural stone in the shower, and a walk-in closet large enough to be another bedroom. It was peaceful. Healing.

Back downstairs, she headed to the kitchen in search of water. The air was warm—no AC, apparently—but she didn't mind as much anymore. The light that poured through the windows made up for it. It warmed her skin, her chest. It felt... alive.

The beds were made. The closets were stocked. There were even clean towels in the bathroom linen closet. This wasn't just a renovation, it was a handoff. Uncle Brian had prepared this place for her.

On the kitchen counter, an envelope waited. Her name, written in Uncle Brian's careful handwriting, sat in neat script across the front.

Jenny picked it up with reverent hands. She poured herself a glass of water and carried both into the living room, pausing again to admire the light that danced across the floor.

This place was more than a house. It was a message. A lifeline.

As she sat down onto the couch, she scanned the living room, noticing the large fireplace, and again, windows on every wall. Jenny turned the envelope over and over in her hands, feeling the thickness of the letter, and an overwhelming feeling of sadness came over her, not just for Uncle Brian, but for herself as well. Uncle Brian's handwriting was easy to recognize on the front:

My Dearest Jenny

A memory came rushing back—sharp, vivid, and unstoppable. Jenny was ten years old, walking home from school on a crisp autumn afternoon when she spotted the big red pickup truck parked in front of her house. It was unmistakable: the silver lettering on the door read **Ritter Brothers Construction**. Uncle Brian's truck. Her father's truck, in contrast, had been silver with red lettering. The difference seemed small, but that day it loomed like a warning.

As she stepped onto the porch, a strange sensation washed over her. At the time, she hadn't had a name for it—just a tightening in her chest, an uneasy flutter in her stomach. Looking back, she understood it for what it was: *foreboding*. A silent alarm ringing in her bones, telling her something was wrong before anyone said a word.

When she opened the front door, the feeling intensified. The living room was filled with people—faces she didn't recognize, their voices hushed, their eyes avoiding hers. The light seemed dimmer somehow, like the whole house had exhaled and gone still. The air was heavy with something she didn't yet understand: grief.

Uncle Brian stepped forward from the circle of adults, his face pale, his eyes rimmed red. He knelt beside the couch and gently guided her to sit next to him. She could still remember how rough the fabric of the sofa felt beneath her small hands, the way his arm wrapped around her shoulders like a protective shield.

He took a deep breath, steadying himself.

"Jenny, honey…" he began, his voice barely holding together. "I have some bad news."

Her breath caught. She didn't know what he was about to say, but every part of her already knew it wasn't good. She stared at him, her heart thudding in her chest like it wanted to run away.

"Your mom and dad... they were in a terrible accident this morning."

His words floated in the air for a moment, hanging like thick fog.

"They... they didn't make it. I'm so sorry, Jenny."

Tears welled in his eyes and finally spilled over. Jenny felt her own begin to rise, not fully understanding, but grasping enough. Her whole world tilted on its axis. Her parents—gone. Just like that. The house, once full of laughter and routine, felt hollow. Foreign.

Uncle Brian tightened his grip around her shoulders. His voice softened.

"But I want you to know something, sweetheart. Everything's going to be OK. I promise. I'll take care of you."

At the time, she didn't know how he could possibly make that promise. How could anyone know what "OK" even looked like after something like this? How could he understand what she needed to feel safe, or whole, or anything close to normal?

And yet... when she looked into his eyes—eyes brimming with pain but also certainty—she believed him.

Uncle Brian and her father had built their business together. They weren't just brothers by blood; they were partners, best friends, each other's second half. He had loved her parents with everything he had, and he loved her, too. She could see that now—clear as day, even through her tears.

That moment, nestled under his arm on the worn living room couch, was the beginning of something new. A quiet understanding passed between them.

He wasn't just offering her comfort. He was making a vow. And for the rest of his life, he never broke it.

She looked at the envelope again, and somehow, without even breaking the seal, she already knew what it would say. Just like fifteen years ago, Uncle Brian had made sure she would be taken care of. That quiet confidence in him had never wavered—not when her world had first fallen apart, and not now. But the thought of opening the letter felt like reopening the wound of losing him. It wasn't just paper and ink inside—it was finality. It was goodbye. And after the long drive and the emotional weight of the day, Jenny didn't feel ready for that. She gently set the envelope on the fireplace mantel, telling herself she'd get to it later, when her heart wasn't quite so raw.

She climbed the stairs slowly, needing a moment alone to collect herself—and maybe splash some cold water on her face. The icy shock grounded her, offering a momentary reprieve from the swirl of emotion threatening to drown her. She reached for a towel, patting her face dry, when her eyes were drawn again to the doorframe in the hallway—the one place in the house untouched by fresh paint.

The faded pencil lines were faint but still legible. Carefully recorded height marks stretched upward, each one labeled with initials: "PJ" and "Ginny." They began low to the ground, the two names side by side, until only one continued past a certain point.

Jenny stepped closer, drawn in by the small and deliberate etchings of someone else's childhood. She traced a fingertip over the timeworn wood, feeling the tiny grooves as if they held echoes of laughter and the quiet rhythm of growing up. Someone had once loved these children enough to track every inch they grew. That small detail, left untouched, felt sacred.

As she grazed her fingers over the scared markings, a flicker of memory stirred, rising from somewhere deep in her mind and heart—ghostly, just out of reach. She could almost hear the laughter of two children, calling each other by special, made-up names only they understood, "JayJay!" "Gin-Gin!". It felt warm, familiar. But just as quickly as it surfaced, the moment slipped away, like a dream evaporating in the morning light.

She wondered who PJ and Ginny had been—siblings, perhaps? Or childhood friends raised under this roof? And why had the renovation crew left this one thing behind? Was it just forgotten? Or did Uncle Brian ask them to preserve it on purpose? It was the kind of question only he could answer—and now, she'd never know.

A quiet ache bloomed in her chest. She hadn't had this kind of normal—this kind of rooted, steady life. Even before the accident, her childhood had always felt like it was waiting for the other shoe to drop. But Uncle Brian... he'd tried. He was always there. Maybe not perfect, but present. Steady. Unshakable. And now, even in his absence, he had given her something lasting. Not just the house. But the quiet message between the lines: *You're still not alone.*

She remembered second grade—one particular Monday afternoon that had stayed lodged in her memory like a splinter. Her classmate, Lance Bingham, had just celebrated his birthday over the weekend. After school, he had proudly invited a few kids to his house to show off his favorite gift: a brand-new checkerboard. Lance boasted that he'd been practicing all weekend and challenged anyone to beat him for a quarter.

Lance wasn't well-liked. His flaming red hair and pale freckled skin made him an easy target for teasing, and his quick temper didn't help his case. He was often the aggressor, using his anger like a shield to hide how much the other kids got under his skin.

Still, five of them followed him home, quarters in hand, drawn by the chance to knock him down a peg. Brent played first and lost almost immediately. He handed over his quarter with a smirk, clearly disappointed but too proud to show it. The rest watched closely, rooting for each other with quiet murmurs that grew louder and more hopeful with every turn. Even if just one of them won, it would feel like a victory for them all.

Jenny was the last to play. She hadn't meant to go last—nerves, probably—but the pressure felt heavier with every match. She wasn't exactly a checkers prodigy. She'd played a few games with Uncle Brian when he came over for dinner, and he always told her she was getting pretty good. Still, she sometimes wondered whether she won because of her skill, or because Uncle Brian let her.

She sat across from Lance, the checkerboard between them, the weight of every other kid's hope resting silently on her shoulders. She didn't care about the quarter. It was the moment—the anticipation, the possibility—that made her want to win.

Their game dragged on longer than any of the others. Piece by piece, the board cleared until they each had just two kinged checkers, chasing each other in circles like tiny hunters. Then, in a sudden stroke of luck and instinct, Jenny saw her opening. She moved fast, capturing both of Lance's final pieces in one smooth swoop.

The room erupted. The kids behind her cheered, arms raised, bouncing in victory. Jenny barely had time to smile before the mood shifted.

Lance's face turned crimson. Whether from embarrassment or rage, she couldn't tell—but she knew something ugly was coming. With a snarl, he flipped the checkerboard into the air and shouted, "Yeah? Well at least my parents love me enough to throw me a birthday party! Jenny's real parents didn't even want her—they gave her away! She's adopted!"

Silence fell like a dropped curtain. The cheers died. The other kids gaped at Jenny, blinking, searching her face for confirmation or denial. But Jenny wasn't sure what to say— because she didn't even know what *adopted* meant.

Her chest tightened. Her eyes stung. She turned and ran— bolted out of the house, her coat clutched in one hand, her boots thudding against the pavement. She didn't stop to look both ways at intersections. She didn't care. She just needed to get home. She needed answers.

When she burst through the front door, Uncle Brian was in the kitchen, making himself a sandwich. He must've been on a nearby job site—sometimes he dropped by for lunch when he was working close.

"Jenny, honey—what's wrong?" he asked, rushing over to her, lifting her onto one of the kitchen stools.

Her voice trembled. "The kids were mean! Lance said I was... I was '*adopted*.' Is it true? What's *adopted* mean, Uncle Brian?"

He paused, scratching his head, clearly caught off guard. "Well," he said gently, "it means your mommy's tummy didn't work quite right. You remember Cindy, from next door?"

Jenny nodded. She remembered Cindy's big belly, the way everyone fussed over her, and how weird the hospital smelled when they went to visit.

"Well, your mommy's tummy couldn't grow a baby like Cindy's. So, your mom and dad found you at an orphanage. That's a place where babies and kids live when they don't have a family yet. They picked *you* out and brought you home."

Jenny tried to understand. It made some sense, though it still left questions.

Uncle Brian knelt in front of her, placing a warm hand on her knee. "Instead of growing in your mommy's tummy," he said, "you grew in her heart. They *chose* you, Jenny. Being adopted isn't something to be ashamed of. It's a blessing. It means you were wanted."

Even back then, long before tragedy struck, Uncle Brian had stepped in to take care of her.

Now, standing in the hallway of the old house he left behind, her hand still brushing the faded pencil lines of "PJ" and

"Ginny," the sadness from before softened. The ache gave way to warmth, and Jenny smiled—really smiled—for the first time since the funeral.

Once again, Uncle Brian had made sure everything would be okay.

~ 3 ~

Shadow and Light

February, 2029

Once her curiosity inside the house had been satisfied, Jenny stepped back outside. The sun was high, casting a warm, golden glow across the landscape—it had already been a long day, and it was only 2pm. She began walking north, following the fence line as it stretched toward the edge of the woods. The property spanned ten acres in total, the house, barn, and shed occupying just a small portion near the southern edge. The rest was open pasture, gently rolling and quiet, split down the middle by a winding creek that flowed from east to west, cutting a serene path through the land.

The further most northeast corner was wooded with birch trees. The pasture held about three-tenths of the grove, and the rest of the trees grew northward. It looked a bit strange for a fence to dramatically cut into a forest like that. Or perhaps, did the forest grow into the pasture?

When she came to the first trees, she heard the faint whinny of a horse; so faint Jenny thought maybe the wind was playing tricks on her. A moment later, she heard it again, a soft sad whinny. She entered the perimeter of the grove, and the air immediately became thick and heavy; the sound of the woods whispered away, no birds chirped, no wind was felt, no crunch of leaves, until there was only silence, except the sounds of the horse. It was surreal, like being in a vacuum; it reminded her of lying under water in her uncle's iron tub, so heavy the claw feet scratched the porcelain tiles beneath; she could hear the sounds, but they were muffled.

She climbed the fence and walked further into the woods, and silently crept along a path towards the sounds, and after about 45-minutes, came upon a mare and her two foals. The mare was tied to a tree and lying on the ground, in obvious distress. Someone brought the mare into the woods and tied her to the tree, her two foals following her there, and staying by her side. They were too young to have been weaned, so the ultimate conclusion was something Jenny didn't want to think about; it was a death sentence for the mare, as well as her two foals. She wanted to scream out, to get help, but her voice wouldn't come. Whatever noise she wanted to make, her body would not allow it. It felt like the grove suppressed all sounds, even hers.

As Jenny quietly crept closer to the horses, not wanting to startle the foals into running, the colors of her surroundings all faded to black, white and gray. The grass, the sun, the green leaves, all turned shades of gray. Even the horses themselves turned an ashy color, or lack of color. She was in a cone of colorless, soundless void. She couldn't comprehend what was happening, so she turned her attention to the horses.

She knelt next to the mare's head, stroking her neck and making soft cooing noises, moving closer to her face, and put her hand gently over her eye. She wanted to soothe her, to help her, to take away the pain she was obviously in. The mare trusted Jenny enough to take a deep breath. The foals slowly walked towards her, their heads low to the ground, sniffing Jenny as they got closer. The mare's breathing slowed, and she died, right there in her arms, before Jenny could even untie her.

Jenny sat motionless, not quite knowing what to do. The foals whinnied softly, waking her from her trance, opening up the void of soundlessness that had enveloped Jenny. Something in her made her legs move; and as she turned around to run back to the barn, the colors immediately came back to life. Although the sounds were still muffled, she could make out the colors of the spring green leaves, the brown dirt path, the green grass, once she crossed over the fence and came to her pasture. She went into the barn and looked around for something she could use to help guide the two foals back.

She found two ropes hanging in the tack room and quickly retraced her steps. As she re-entered the grove, the familiar hush fell over her again—sounds softened, almost muted—but the colors remained just as vivid as before. Strangely, the foals didn't bolt at her approach. Instead, they turned toward their mother and let out soft, uncertain whinnies, then allowed Jenny to gently lead them away. Navigating back through the thick woods to reach the main path was a struggle, but the foals followed without resistance, as if they instinctively understood they were being led somewhere safe, somewhere they would be cared for.

Jenny led the foals into one of the larger stalls and immediately began scanning the barn for the supplies she knew she'd need. Unfortunately, the barn was not as well-stocked as the house. She found a few things she could use; a few squared bundles of shavings. So, she threw in a fresh layer of wood chips to make them comfortable, though she knew they were too young to eat hay or oats. There wasn't much more she could do on her own, these foals needed medical attention. Pulling out her phone, she quickly searched online for a nearby veterinarian. The first number rang with no answer, and the second and third were both disconnected, each failed call tightening the knot of urgency in her chest.

On the fourth try, the call finally connected. Dr. Paul Payne from Kitty Hawk Vet Services picked up, his calm voice instantly reassuring Jenny that she'd done the right thing. But when she gave him the address, there was a pause—a noticeable hesitation. She could almost hear the wheels turning in his mind, as if the location stirred a memory or unease he wasn't ready to voice.

"I'm not sure I can come, right now. How about I give you the number of another vet?"

"I've already called three other vets, and they all either didn't answer or were disconnected." Jenny was not just irritated, but pleading for this man to come. "Please, there's no one else."

She felt him hesitate once more, and finally Dr. Payne resigned to the knowledge that there really was no one else in the area. He assured her that he would come by as soon as he could, and they hung up.

Jenny spent the time rummaging around in the barn and shed for items she thought she would need, making a mental list of items to purchase after the vet came and went. Having worked previously at a high-end barn, she knew the basic items she would need to have stocked.

When Dr. Payne arrived, Jenny couldn't help but find it amusing how his appearance didn't match the voice she'd heard over the phone. He had sounded much older—seasoned and serious—but in person, he looked to be around her age, maybe mid-twenties. She hadn't picked up on the subtle Native American lilt in his voice during their call, but it was unmistakable in person. His features reflected his heritage: smooth, dark skin, jet-black hair, and almond-shaped eyes. But what stood out most were those eyes—their unusual gray-blue hue was striking, almost otherworldly. Beautiful, yes, but undeniably unexpected. "Dr. Payne," Jenny started.

"Please, call me Paul," he replied.

"OK, Paul. Thanks so much for coming. I didn't know what else to do." Jenny felt the need to explain, but he waved her off and started for the barn.

He did a thorough workup of the twin foals and gave them a clean bill of health. They were a bit dehydrated but were in good health otherwise.

Paul contacted the local animal shelter and requested that someone come out to assess the situation. It wasn't long before a truck pulled up and a woman stepped out—Mary Coleman, the director of the Beechland Animal Shelter. Jenny found herself caught off guard. Mary didn't look anything like what she'd imagined an animal welfare director would. Not that she had a clear picture in mind, but whatever she'd expected, it wasn't this.

First, she was short, she was only 5'3". Her thick red hair cascaded down her back to her waist, which made Jenny a bit jealous. She was in her fifties, but her eyes sparkled a pale blue, and her smile was genuine. It was obvious that she truly loved what she did.

Mary's old truck, on the other hand, was exactly what Jenny imagined a nonprofit director might drive. It had probably been white once, but now it was coated in a thick layer of dust, giving it a taupe-gray hue that begged for someone to scrawl "wash me" on the tailgate. The right front fender stood out in faded, oxidized blue—clearly a replacement—and, ironically, it was the only part of the truck with a dent.

"Hi Mary, thanks for coming." Paul gave her a quick kiss on the cheek. Jenny thought it was odd, but whatever. "Like I said on the phone, the mare was tied to a tree in the grove behind the property." They all started towards the barn. "These two little ones were left alone, until Jenny here stopped by. Why did you stop by, can I ask?"

"Well, I'm the new owner of the property. I just showed up this afternoon and I heard the… commotion. I just followed the sounds."

Paul gave her an odd look. "Well, OK then." They came to the stall with the foals and Mary walked right in, needing no invitation.

"Aren't these guys beautiful? It's too bad they've had such a rough start in life." She quietly and calmly stroked their necks.

"What do you think Mary? Do you have room at the facility for these little guys?" Paul had a hopeful look on his face.

"Unfortunately, no," Mary's eyes saddened. "And all my fosters are full up, as well. It's baby season after all! How about you, can you take them back to your place? Or how about Kimber?"

Paul sighed heavily. "Now Mary, you know I can't take on foals this young. They need feeding every three hours, I'm on the road more than I am at home. And Kimber, well, not only does she not have a barn, but her head is more into her wedding these days. I don't think she'd be the best person for the job."

Both Mary and Paul looked at Jenny, together, as if it were planned. She could feel a major guilt trip coming her way and immediately put up her hands. "Oh no... I may not know you two very well, but I know what you guys are thinking. I just got here today. I was planning on selling the place. I don't even live here!"

Mary's eyes softened. "I can come by every day to help out. The Beechland Shelter will pay for all the food and medical supplies the foals need. I'll make some calls to see if there is a nurse mare in the area, or another mare that may have lost their foal."

"And I guess you can count on me to be here as well." Jenny could tell that Paul was giving in to something he really didn't want to. But he knew Jenny needed some convincing.

Jenny looked at the foals, watching them rubbing their noses on Mary's back, like an itch they couldn't reach. Damnit if they weren't too cute! It was a conspiracy; she just knew it. She took a deep breath, "Fine, alright. I'll need help, and right away."

Mary and Paul looked at each other, a knowing glance between them. *Another sucker born every day!* Jenny could feel them think to each other.

They immediately went into high gear, walking from room to room in the barn, making a list of supplies needed, making calls to people for help. Both of them went to their prospective trucks, coming back with supplies that they had on hand. Before they left, Jenny had a tack room with several halters, leads, and buckets of all sizes, and a storage room full of bottles and cleaning supplies for them.

While Mary went back to the shelter, Paul gave Jenny a tutorial for feeding the youngsters. They were pretty hungry by that time, so it was a very messy and funny demonstration. More formula ended up on them than in the foals.

The twins were Appaloosa, like their mother. The filly was white with black spots on her rump, the colt was black with white spots, total and complete opposites. Jenny decided to call them Yin and Yang, the Chinese symbol for Shadow and Light, meaning duality, but one cannot exist without the other.

At the beginning of this very long day, Jenny was all alone, until she wasn't.

~ ~ * ~ ~

After Paul and Mary left, Jenny made the decision to stay in that home and not put the house and property up for sale. After all, Uncle Brian wanted her there, and now that the foals needed looking after, there was a purpose for her being there.

True to her word, Mary stopped by every day for the next three weeks, and she never came empty-handed, always bringing supplies for the twins, or a volunteer to help with the barn. One day she even brought along a three-legged dog. The dog was one of Mary's *many treasures*, as she called them. Gems that were discovered after being uncovered in the rough, or rather saved from less than savory circumstances. Tripod was a golden retriever who had been hit by a car. Unfortunately, he didn't have a license tag, or micro-chip, so the owner was never found. His front right leg was completely shattered and would never heal from the accident; removal was necessary for his survival.

Not many people wanted to adopt animals with health issues, or are less than perfect, so Mary and other staff members ended up taking most of them home. Tripod was Mary's favorite dog. The first time Jenny saw him, he bounced out of the truck with a very strange jump. As awkward as he looked, he was very agile. And his attitude was as great as most dogs she'd known. He was happy, jumping up onto every person he saw, his tail wagging like a tangled fishing line trying to get free.

A few days later, Mary showed up with even more help. "Hey Mary." Jenny nodded as Mary's truck pulled in.

"Hey Jenny. Kirsten and Linda are sisters," she introduced a young woman, probably 18, blond, perfect body, beautiful face. "Kirsten is one of the volunteers at the shelter. Thought I'd bring her by today, she said she'd love to help with the twins." Kirsten walked into the barn, looking for her new charges, not stopping to say hello. "Well, I guess she's a bit excited."

Then, another girl slowly climbed out of Mary's big truck. She was small, round, and had Down Syndrome. She walked right up to Jenny and hugged her. "Hello, my name is Linda. How are you? What is your name?" Linda asked, without taking a breath, making it sound like one long run-on sentence.

"Linda, this is Jenny. This is her barn. She is in charge of the horses," Mary informed.

"May I see the horses?" Jenny could see the sparkle in her eye, asking permission to visit the very animals she cared about. She already loved her.

"Of course you can!" Jenny said and whisked her away to the barn.

Kirsten was already in Yin and Yang's stall, trying to get them to settle down, they were very excited to see new people. "Kristen, why don't you try feeding them," Jenny said, bringing her a bottle.

"It's Kirsten, NOT Kristen." There was no malice in her voice, merely annoyance, she just wanted to make sure Jenny knew her name; she'd probably had trouble with that in the past.

The foals were both fighting for the one bottle as Mary gave another one to Linda. "Here, why don't you try to feed the white one there, her name is Yin."

Linda slowly opened the stall, flinching as both the foals went to her looking for their meal. Kirsten took Yang by his halter and showed him the bottle, and he took to it, as Yin went to the bottle offered in front of her. Linda immediately laughed, loving the attention she got from the tiny foal.

"They'll be by every day during the week for two months," Mary informed Jenny. "Kirsten is working towards being a vet, and this looks good on her resume'. And Linda, well she just loves horses, and since the Beechland Animal Shelter doesn't have the facility for horses, I thought I'd send you a little help."

"Wonderful! I can use all the help I can get," replied Jenny. "Thanks for bringing them by!"

Both foals had settled down, loving the fact they each had their own person feeding them, instead of the usual one person, making them fight for affection as they fed.

As Jenny and Mary were walking out of the barn, Mary asked, "So, Jenny, I've been dying to ask you. How did you ever get Paul to come over?" Mary was too curious to be apologetic.

"What do you mean? He's a vet, I had an animal problem, isn't that his job?"

"Well, what I mean is, I was surprised he didn't have someone else take the call. See, this used to be his home. He grew up here. His dad lost the place to the bank about a year ago. I'm pretty sure it was difficult for him to see someone else living here."

"Gosh, that would explain the hesitation he gave me. But I didn't tell him I lived here when I called. I just told him I found the foals in the grove behind the house."

~ ~ * ~ ~

Two weeks later, Mary brought another rescue to the barn.

"This is Zaar Aza," Mary explained to Jenny as she unloaded the handsome old bay Thoroughbred. "He's an ex-racehorse, 28, retired. He won big and made a lot of money for his owner. His owner, Dale is one of the good ones. He kept Zaar Aza all his life after retiring him from racing. He didn't ship him off to an auction and possible slaughter like so many people do when their horses no longer make them money. Unfortunately, Dale was just diagnosed with stage four lung cancer and is in hospice right now. They don't think Dale's gonna make it much longer. I just need a quick transitional place to keep him until I find a permanent home for him."

Jenny smiled. She was more than happy to take on another horse. Yin and Yang were rambunctious, but Jenny was comfortable now. She had settled into her home a while ago, and into a nice routine with the foals. The prospect of another horse wasn't so scary. She had Mary and Paul for support, as well as Linda and Kirsten.

~ 4 ~

Journal of Eleanor Dare
1588 - 1604

The 25th Day of September, 1588
Manteo, once again, has been our savior. Two days past, as we were moving our scant supplies from the Cittie of Raleigh to dwell with the Croatoan people, a sudden cry pierced the stillness behind us in the woods. Virginia and I, seized by terror, hid ourselves deep within thick shrubbery, hearts pounding as we beheld the horror unfolding.

From our concealment, we witnessed the Secotan descend upon our company like wolves. The woods echoed with the screams of our friends and kin, and we watched, helpless, as they were struck down with cruel and ruthless hands. The Secotan showed no mercy — men, women, even children were caught in the bloody assault.

For two long days and nights, Virginia and I lay silent and still, too afraid to move lest the Secotan discover us. Hunger gnawed at our bellies, but fear was far greater. We dared not hope for rescue.

Then, as if by divine providence, Manteo came. He had grown uneasy, for our arrival was overdue, and knowing our plight, he searched tirelessly. He found us hiding, and others as well, but the survivors were few. Only thirty-two souls remained from what had been our once proud company.

Our loss is beyond measure. My beloved husband, Ananais, has not been found, and my heart aches with the unbearable weight of his absence. The Croatoan scoured the woods for many days, seeking survivors or signs of the lost, but their search was in vain. I am left to raise Virginia alone in this harsh new world, bereft of the comfort of my husband and the strength of my friends.

Still, my father has not returned. Each passing day without word makes my hope dwindle, yet Manteo urges us to move the Croatoan village once more, warning that the Secotan's wrath will not rest. With heavy hearts, we took up our journey anew. Though lighter in burden and fewer in number, we travel swiftly, knowing that safety lies in distance and caution.

Winter, 1589

This bitter winter is the cruelest yet. I have abandoned all hope of ever finding Ananais alive. The cold presses upon my spirit as much as the land. Yet Virginia, now two years old, grows strong and bright. She flourishes despite the hardship, learning both Algonquin, the language of the Croatoan, and English from those who still speak it.

Though many of the children perished, others survived the Secotan's savage strike, and Virginia has playmates to keep her company in these long, dark days.

Our numbers have dwindled to but thirty-two souls — barely a quarter of those who first set foot in this New World. We now live wholly among the Croatoan, sharing in their customs and their strength.

Still, my father's fate remains a mystery. No word comes from England, and I fear he has been lost to the sea or worse.

Spring, 1589
To endure, several English women who lost their husbands have taken Croatoan men as their own. Seven now carry new life within them. It gladdens my heart to know that soon, laughter and cries of babes will fill our village once more. These children shall be a symbol of hope and renewal, born of two worlds intertwined.

Winter, 1590
The Secotan do not relent in their war against us. They stalk us like shadows, slaying our livestock and burning our crops. The Croatoan live in constant motion, fleeing from one place to another to avoid the savage attacks.

I do not know how much more hardship Virginia and I can endure. At three years of age, this cruel life weighs heavily on such a small child, yet she shows a resilience beyond her years.

Spring, 1595

Virginia is growing swiftly, her spirit as lively as the spring itself. She now speaks Algonquin with the ease of her Croatoan companions, far more fluently than English. Her love for all creatures of the earth is boundless, but none capture her heart as deeply as the horses.

There is one in particular—a small white mare flecked with black spots. Virginia spends hours with her, whispering secrets and sharing quiet moments. The mare is her closest companion, and their bond seems as old as the land itself.

Spring, 1604

I have grown very ill, and fear this may be my last entry. The fever has ravaged me these many weeks, and though the healer has done all within her power, I feel my strength fading.

I have done my best to raise Virginia, and she is now sixteen—a fine and gracious young lady. My deepest wish for her is a life filled with happiness and peace, free from the sorrows I have known.

My only regret is that she has never met her father, Ananais, nor her grandfather. I pray that someday she may know their names and their stories, and that our lineage will endure in this strange new land.

~ 5 ~
Snookie

March, 2029

Dew clung to the grass like diamonds scattered across the field. When Yin and Yang burst into the pasture, their hooves carved dark tracks through the wet blades, splashing their legs

Yin flitted forward, attempting a trot, but her too-long legs tangled beneath her. She surged into a slow, graceful lope—fluid as water, her tail held high like a banner. Head up, she sniffed the sweet spring air, then drifted to a stop near the creek and dropped her head to graze, content.

Where Yin was elegance in motion, Yang was chaos on legs. He bolted along the fence line, also trying to trot, but his lanky limbs betrayed him. With a squeal and a buck, he gave in to a full gallop, testing the limits of his growing body. Reaching the creek, he attempted a dramatic leap, but ended up splashing straight through. After a full loop of the pasture, he skidded to a halt in front of the barn, then trotted over to his sister.

He nipped at her rear—ever the pest—but she gave him a swift buck in warning. Undeterred, he circled her. They ended up nose to nose. Jenny imagined Yin saying, *"I'm the boss. You're the dork."*

It was clear who'd been born first.

The rest of the day, they grazed within ten feet of each other, never straying far.

Zaar Aza, meanwhile, was settling in without fuss. Introduced to the twins, he barely flicked an ear. He had that "been there, done that" energy—steady and unbothered. Each morning, he ate his breakfast, spent the day grazing, and returned to the barn on his own. He moved slower than the twins, his age showing in the stiffness of his gait. Jenny did some research and added Glucosamine to his feed. It helped, though he was still creaky in the mornings.

But he was content. That was enough.

~ ~ * ~ ~

After two weeks of all-night feedings, no sleep and fast food, Jenny finally had her first opportunity to walk back to the grove where the foals were found. Mary had one of her contacts come out the day after the foals were found and take care of the mare. They had buried her inside the pasture near the grove. Jenny felt it was appropriate. It felt as though the mare finally had a home, and now it was permanent.

The instant she took the first step into the forest, the air grew still. She no longer heard the chirps of birds, the wind through the leaves, or her own breath. It was as if a sound-proof void had suddenly enveloped the grove. The air was heavy, thick, and full of memory. Immediately she felt the temperature dip 10 degrees, even though the sun was still high.

Although the trees were young at the outer edge, they were still about 20 years old. Something felt odd; she noticed there was a pattern to the path, or rather *felt* the pattern, and followed it to better understand it. The trees grew in a circular pattern, which wound its way to the middle of the grove, like a snail's shell. The grove got smaller and smaller as it grew to the center, as the trees grew older, larger.

The path was clean and smooth, no brush or rock jutted into the trail, it was as if someone had graded the whole grove before planting. They were all birch trees, but the largest tree in the very middle of the grove had what appeared to be a buffalo etched into its trunk, about 6 feet from the ground. She wondered who put the carvings on the trees, and for what purpose? She had no idea what the carvings meant and made a promise to herself to do more research.

~ ~ * ~ ~

One evening Jenny drove to Beechland for a much-needed treat. Nothing beats an iced caramel macchiato from Starbucks after an unseasonably hot spring day.

She drove through the small one-stoplight town, and pulled into the one and only diner, *Dannie's Diner,* which promised "The BEST Rhubarb Pie in Virginia!" *No Starbucks, damn!* She thought.

The rich aroma of freshly brewed coffee wafted through the air as she stepped inside, the small bell above the door chiming to announce her arrival. The diner was a textbook throwback to the 1960s—a true blast from the past. From the entrance, the layout wrapped around both sides of a gleaming stainless-steel bar, flanked by rotating stools upholstered in glossy candy-apple red vinyl. The walls were lined with large windows, each booth tucked neatly along the perimeter, matching the stools in their bold red upholstery. Sleek black tables with polished chrome edging completed the retro look, and beneath it all, a classic black-and-white checkered floor stretched from wall to wall, adding the perfect finishing touch to the vintage vibe.

Jenny walked to the counter and waited for the waitress to look up from the novel she was reading; it must have been a slow evening.

The rather large woman looked up as she turned a page, flashed Jenny a smile and folded the corner of the page she had just turned. "Hey there! What can I get ya, Hon?"

"Do you have flavored coffees?" Jenny desperately missed her Starbucks back in Boston. Whenever she walked through the door, the barista immediately knew what she wanted: iced coffee caramel macchiato. They even knew her car and had the drink ready in the drive thru.

"Sure do!" the waitress said. "What's your poison?"

When Jenny gave her order, she truly expected the waitress to look at her as if she was an alien, but she whipped around to the espresso machine and deftly made the drink. She turned and gave Jenny the drink. "Say, don't I know you? You look really familiar."

"Probably not. I just moved here from Boston about a couple months ago." Jenny smiled.

"Well, welcome to Beechland! I'm Dannie," she said with a warm, easy smile. It didn't take long to see that she was the heart of the place—her energy and charm clearly one of the main reasons the diner was so beloved.

It was nearing sundown by the time Jenny left the diner, the fading light casting long shadows and softening the landscape. As she rounded the final corner before her driveway, something on the side of the road caught her eye—movement, low and unsteady. She slowed the car and came to a stop, squinting into the dim light. It was a raccoon, clearly injured and struggling. A fresh blood trail showed it had dragged itself to the shoulder, likely after being struck by a car. Its head was badly injured—its lower jaw grotesquely dislocated and hanging loosely. One front paw was mangled, barely recognizable. If the animal survived, it would almost certainly need an amputation.

Jenny grabbed a blanket from the car and carefully scooped up the injured creature, wrapping it gently in the soft fabric. The drive from the highway to her house took another ten minutes, and she went slowly, avoiding potholes and bumps. As she turned onto her long driveway, something strange happened—the colors around her began to fade, gradually shifting into shades of black and white. It was so subtle she didn't notice until, just as she reached the house, color rushed back into the world, as if someone had flipped a switch.

She laid the raccoon gently on the kitchen counter, but it was too late—the animal had died in her arms. Yet as she stood there in stunned silence, she noticed something: a small movement in the raccoon's belly. Then another. Horror gripped her as realization dawned—she was pregnant. The lump twitched again, and a wave of nausea and dread washed over Jenny as she understood what had to be done if the babies were to survive.

It wasn't a decision, it was instinct. She picked up her phone and called Paul, silently praying he was nearby. But he was two hours away. They didn't have time to wait. So, they settled on what could only be called "surgery by phone."

Jenny had never performed anything like this. Her work with animals had always come after the trauma—rehabilitation, not rescue. Seeing pain this raw, this immediate, left her shaken and unsure. But as Paul talked her through each step, she pushed her fear aside and focused, determined to give those babies a chance at life.

"It'll be OK, Jenny. I'll hold your hand, metaphorically, through the whole thing," he laughed. It was his way of lightening the mood, but it didn't work, Jenny was still terrified. "OK, so get the following items to get set up."

Paul gave her a list, and she frantically searched throughout the house looking for the 'surgery' tools. A few items had to be improvised, such as a heat lamp, but there was a heating pad to keep the kits warm after they were born. Also, there wasn't a nasal aspirator available, so a turkey baster would have to do. Since the mother had already passed, there was a lot of prep Jenny didn't need to do, but antiseptic was still a necessity. She hoped Purell would work.

"So, first, sterilize EVERYTHING," Paul said. "We don't want the babies to get an infection. They'll have a rough enough start in life as it is." Jenny did what she was told, cleaning the kitchen counter, the tools and the mother as best she could. Paul walked her through how to do the incision, and she was quite surprised with herself at how easy it was to do the most disgusting of procedures. She was able to gently remove two babies.

"They aren't moving!" she uttered, and began to panic.

"Slow down, it's OK. First, wipe them down; make sure their airways are clear." The towel was used to clear the gunk away from their mouths and face. Then the turkey baster was used (very carefully) to clean out their mouths and noses. One kit immediately started squealing. Jenny wrapped it up in a blanket she had warmed in the microwave and went to work on the other, smaller one.

Jenny feverishly tried everything Paul told her to do, from rubbing the body, to aspirating the nose and mouth, but was unable to revive the little one. She felt like an utter failure. Tears welled up as she told him the baby was gone. "It's OK, Jenny. You did the best you could. It was probably just too small. Let's concentrate on the one that made it. Tell me the sex." Paul explained how to check, it was a little girl.

Paul congratulated Jenny on her first delivery and said he would get there as soon as he was done with his current appointment. He assured her that the kit would be fine for a few hours, provided she was kept warm and safe.

Jenny took her to the living room, sat down and cradled the kit under her shirt to keep warm. She suckled on her little finger as Jenny stroked her fur. The kit would need to feed soon;

hopefully Paul would make it back in time. The kit was absolutely adorable. Even as little as she was, her bandit face gave her a mischievous look. Her hands were little gloved fingers that wrapped around Jenny's pinky as she sucked on it.

Once Paul arrived, he performed his examination, and declared the kit perfectly healthy, if a bit dehydrated. He left a case of baby formula specially made for small mammals and went on with his evening. Jenny named her Snookie.

~ 6 ~

Stray Cat Strut

April, 2029

Two weeks later Mary stopped by to check on Yin and Yang, but she didn't arrive empty handed. In her arms she had a small bundle of black fluff. The six-week-old kitten had been abandoned at the shelter. Her fur was very fine and fluffy, her tail was too long for her body, and her ears were too large for her triangle face, the shape of which made her resemble a long-tailed bat.

Jenny's first instinct was to shake her head and turn the kitten away; she'd had enough experiences go bad in her life with this sort of thing. Like the first time Uncle Brian came home with a pet. It was about a month after her parents had died. She was having a hard time adjusting to her new home, as well as her new school. It was difficult making friends, on top of losing her parents. The teachers in her school were prepped with the information, so they could give Jenny extra attention if needed, but the other kids had no idea what was going on. She was just another new kid in school.

Uncle Brian came home one day with a beautiful Australian Shepherd Border Collie mix. He had one blue eye, almost white, and one brown eye. He was such a mix of black and white; you couldn't tell if he was black with white spots, or white with black spots, but you definitely could not call him gray.

Uncle Brian picked him out from the local animal shelter, knowing how important it was to rescue animals, rather than perpetuate the horrific cycle of puppy mills. His name was Rocky, and he knew it well. He wasn't a puppy, and with that came the calmness of realizing he was safe, and home.

Rocky slept on Jenny's bed every night, making her so hot she usually gave up her blankets halfway through the night. He waited at the door every day for Jenny when it was time for her to come home from school.

Six months after they got Rocky, Jenny came home from school, and he wasn't at the door. She instinctively knew something was wrong. Rocky was always at the door, always, without fail, every day. She ran to her room, *Maybe he was taking a nap, and lost track of time,* at least that's what she thought. But he wasn't there. Jenny looked all over the house but couldn't find him.

She checked outside in the huge backyard; it was mostly grass, with a few bare spots where Rocky made his circular run around every morning. It was surrounded by bushes that seemed to attract yellow tennis balls they threw for Rocky; Jenny was sure one day a tennis ball tree would sprout up from all the balls it ate. There were several areas in the bushes that had been hollowed out from Rocky digging in for the balls as well. As Jenny walked into the yard, her eyes were drawn immediately to a black and white spot in one of Rocky's favorite napping areas.

As she approached, she knew in her heart it was Rocky. She knew he had died.

She ran inside and hid in her bed, smelling Rocky on the sheets. When Uncle Brian came home, he had to come looking for both Jenny and Rocky, as neither were at the door waiting for him, as they had done every day for six months. Jenny was so devastated she stayed home from school for three days.

Uncle Brian wanted to know what had happened. Rocky was healthy, and although not young, he wasn't very old either. The doctor who performed the necropsy called with the news. Rocky had a mass in his brain. It had grown so fast he didn't have time to show any symptoms. Rocky appeared healthy, right up until the end; they had no idea he was even sick. He was taken so quickly, he didn't have time to suffer. It was a blessing.

It didn't feel like a blessing to an 11-year-old girl. It felt like a cruel joke.

Mary placed the black fluff-ball in Jenny's hands, and her heart melted. The kitten's big green eyes looked up, so full of adoration and neediness, Jenny didn't want to let her go. She needed to change the subject, to keep her mind off the cute kitten in her arms, so she asked Mary how she became the President of the Beechland Animal Shelter.

"That's a short story but goes back a few years. My twin brother, Josh lived in San Antonio at the time. The company he worked for was sending him to New Orleans for a week, to meet up with some client or something or other. So, we made plans to meet there and spend some time together, sort of a spur of the moment family reunion of sorts. Anyway, he ended up in the hospital with kidney stones the morning of his flight, and wasn't able to contact me before my flight left. I got the message while I was at baggage claim. Since I'd already paid for the trip, I decided to stay in New Orleans and make the most of it.

"Unfortunately, Hurricane Katrina hit. Not only was my vacation ruined, but I couldn't get home. I was watching the news from my hotel, and saw a story about all the animals that had been left behind when their owners fled from the rushing waters. The local authorities were looking for volunteers to help gather them up.

"When the catastrophe was pretty much handled, as far as the animals were concerned, the shelter coordinator in New Orleans asked me to stay on. I told her I lived in Virginia, so she told me that the need for help was all over the country. She made a few calls, and by the time I made it back home, I had a job at Beechland Animal Shelter. I just worked my way up the ladder from there. I started out volunteering, and the rest is history."

~ ~ * ~ ~

As she grew, Misha's coat grew longer, and thicker. She did finally grow into her ears, but her tail still seemed too long for her body. Unlike most cats, when she was happy, her tail would fluff out like a puffin fish when provoked.

58

When Misha and Snookie met, it was love at first sight. Those two tiny balls of fluff became instantly inseparable— playing together, exploring side by side, and curling up together every night. Though they each had their own beds on the floor, they almost always found their way onto Jenny's bed by the middle of the night, nestled close to each other and to her. They did everything as a pair, a perfect little duo from the very beginning.

About two months later, Misha seemed to gain weight overnight. Her little figure took on an odd shape—her belly suddenly round and pronounced, while the rest of her remained slender. When she sat, she looked like a pear-shaped vase, which only added to her charm. She even developed a new trick: sitting upright on her haunches and raising her front paws like a begging statue. It was impossible to resist. One look and treats practically flew her way.

When Misha and Snookie were small, they had a habit of curling up under Jenny's chin as she slept—a sweet, if short-lived phase. After a few sleepless nights, Jenny gently guided them into a new routine, one under each arm. They took to it immediately, finding their own cozy spots. But as Misha grew and her long, luxurious coat filled out, it became too warm to stay nestled against Jenny's side. So, she claimed her own space—stretched out on her back at the foot of the bed, all four legs sticking straight up in the air. It was utterly ridiculous—and absolutely adorable. She looked like a little bear sunning herself, which earned her the nickname "Misha-Bear." Snookie, ever loyal, would always snuggle up next to her—some part of her body touching Misha's, as if tethered by affection.

Every night, they slept with Jenny. And without fail, they woke her each morning at exactly 6 a.m. Jenny never knew whether their internal clocks were tuned to hunger or the sounds of the horses stirring outside—but either way, their timing was impeccable.

Despite her princess-like demeanor, Misha despised the barn. It was beneath her royal sensibilities-too dirty, too noisy, too everything. That's why Jenny was surprised when, one morning, Misha followed her in for the first feeding. Head held high, tail flicking with precision, she tiptoed across the floor, careful to avoid any unsavory mess.

Misha found a clean, quiet corner and settled in to observe. She sat like a small, fuzzy sentinel as Jenny moved through her morning routine. Yin and Yang, now three months old, were the loudest by far—constantly bleating for food, treats, attention, or all of the above. Their names were no accident. Yin was gentle, polite, and reserved—except when she was bossing her brother around. Yang was pure chaos: long-legged, energetic, always moving, always stirring up trouble. They were polar opposites, but inseparable, and Jenny already knew she'd miss them when it came time to say goodbye. She secretly hoped they'd find a new home together.

Then there was Zaar Aza, the wise old soul of the barn. Quiet, patient, steady. He never needed fuss or fanfare—he simply understood. Jenny had always felt like she learned more from him than she could ever teach.

And through it all, every morning, Misha sat in that same quiet corner—watching, listening, waiting.

~ 7 ~

Journal of John White 1590

August 18, 1590

Today, at last, I have returned to the New World. It is my granddaughter Virginia's third birthday—a joyous occasion, made all the more precious by my arrival. I long to surprise her, to hold her in my arms and tell her how dearly I have missed her. I have been away for three long years, far longer than I promised. I vowed to return sooner, bearing supplies, victuals, planters, and more settlers to strengthen our colony. But the cruel tides of war with Spain and a lack of funds delayed my journey.

As I approached the island, the air smelled of smoke and decay. We came upon a fire, where grass and several rotting trees still smoldered, scattered about the clearing as if the land itself mourned the passage of time and struggle. From there, we ventured deeper into the woods, making our way through dense thickets toward the part of the island directly opposite Dasamongwepeuk.

Our journey led us along the water's edge, tracing a wide arc around the northern point of the island. It was a long path, yet one filled with signs—silent marks of the lives that had passed this way.

In the sand, I noticed the prints of feet, the impressions of several sorts of Native peoples, fresh enough to show they had traveled here recently, under the cover of night. I could feel the weight of their presence, watching, waiting, cautious.

Then, at the very edge of a sandy bank, carved deeply into the bark of a large tree, I saw it: the letters C R O. The Roman letters stood clear and deliberate—a secret token, a message from my people.

At my departure in 1587, I had instructed the settlers that if they moved from Roanoke, they should mark the trees or posts of their new settlement with the name of the place. Should they be in distress, they were to carve a cross above the name as a sign of trouble.

But there was no cross.

This meant they were safe, or so I dared hope.

Pressing on, we reached the place where the colony had once thrived, now marked by the remains of several houses. The structures were dismantled, the site enclosed by a strong palisade of tall trees, woven together with curtain walls and flankers, sturdy and fort-like.

Near the entrance stood a chief post with its bark stripped away, and carved clearly into the wood, five feet above the ground, the word CROATOAN—again, without any cross or sign of distress.

With a mixture of relief and dread, we entered the enclosure. Scattered about were iron bars, two pigs of lead, four iron fowlers, iron sacker-shot, and other heavy items left behind, almost swallowed by the wild grass and weeds growing unchecked.

We then followed the water's edge toward the creek's point, hoping to find any sign of their boats or pinnaces. But the water was empty of their craft, and none of the falcons or small ordinance I had left with them remained.

Returning from the creek, some sailors brought troubling news. They had discovered places where several chests had once been hidden—dug up and broken open long ago. Many of the goods were spoiled or scattered, ruined beyond use. It was clear the enemy savages from Dasamongwepeuk had watched our men depart for Croatoan, then looted every suspected hiding place.

Captain Cooke and I went to the site of an old trench, dug two years prior by Captain Amadas. There we found five chests, carefully hidden by the colonists. Three were mine. Around the area, found my belongings desecrated—books torn from their bindings, the frames of pictures and maps rotted by rain, my armor nearly eaten through by rust.

Though I grieved the destruction, my heart leapt with joy upon seeing the clear token that the colony had moved safely to Croatoan—the birthplace of Manteo and the land of our Native friends.

As I explored the surroundings of the fort, I came upon a most curious sight: a pure white tree standing alone in a wide clearing, unlike any other in the forest. Its pale bark gleamed in the sunlight, a stark beacon amid the green and brown.

Upon this tree, I found another carving—an image unlike any I had seen before. It depicted a large, four-legged creature, with a broad head crowned by two impressive horns. The figure was bold, intricate, and mysterious.

I have never seen an animal quite like this, nor a tree so strange and singular. The sight filled me with wonder and unease—what secrets does this land yet hold? What stories remain untold beneath these leaves?

August 18, 1590 (continued)

After we had seen all that we could in that place, we made our way back to our boats, eager to depart from the shore as swiftly as possible. The sky was darkening, heavy clouds rolling in quickly, warning us of an approaching storm. The air grew thick and the wind picked up ominously, promising a foul and stormy night ahead.

With great effort and danger, we managed to get ourselves aboard the ships before nightfall. By then, the wind and the sea had risen fiercely, tossing the vessels with such force that we feared our cables and anchors would not hold firm until morning.

The captain, acting with swift judgment, ordered a small boat to be manned by five strong men, all excellent swimmers. Their mission was to cross to the little island on the right side of the harbor, where six of our men had been filling casks with fresh water. Though the boat returned safely that very night with our men aboard, the heavy casks of fresh water had to be left behind—retrieving them in such tempestuous conditions would have risked the lives of both men and boats. Thus, the night proved fierce and merciless.

August 19, 1590
At dawn, the captain, the master, and I gathered to discuss our next course. The winds were favorable for

sailing to Croatoan, where our planters were believed to be settled. It was also decided to leave the fresh water casks on the island until our return, though the rough seas the previous night had dashed our hopes of retrieving them safely.

As preparations were underway, disaster struck: as the anchor was nearly raised, the cable snapped suddenly. With the loss of a second anchor, we were driven dangerously close to shore, where Kenrick's Mounts loomed. We hastily dropped a third anchor, but the ship was almost grounded. Only by fortunate circumstance did we slip into a deeper channel nearer to the shore than we had realized, narrowly avoiding wreckage.

Yet, the cost was great—we were left with but one anchor and one cable of the four we had brought. The weather grew ever more threatening, provisions dwindled, and fresh water was lost with the casks we left behind.

Faced with these hardships, we resolved to sail southward toward Saint John or another island where fresh water might be found. We also planned that if supplies could be procured at Hispaniola, Saint John, or Trinidad, we would spend the coming winter in the Indies, hoping to make two profitable voyages in one season before returning to Virginia.

The captain and the company aboard the Admiral agreed to this plan, despite my earnest petitions to proceed directly to Croatoan. Our fate, however, hung on the decision of the crew of the Moone-light, our consort. When asked to join us, they declined, citing the weakness and leaks in their ship. Thus, that very night we parted ways—the Moone-light set a course directly for England, while the Admiral headed for Trinidad, a course we followed for two days.

August 20, 1590

Today, under the captain's firm insistence, we resolved to sail for England immediately. The storm clouds gathered, provisions ran dangerously low, and it became clear we would not reach Croatoan as I had so desperately hoped.

Before departing, we left behind a trusted native companion named Kihukee, a man born of these lands and familiar with the people. Into his care, I entrusted this journal. I pray he will find my daughter, Eleanor, and deliver to her these words: that I have searched for her, that I have never ceased to look, and that I will return to find her one day.

Eleanor, my dear Eleanor—my heart aches each day that I left you behind. Now I know, with painful certainty, that I should never have gone.

~ 8 ~

Angels We Have Heard on High

May, 2029

One week later, Mary called. "Hey Jenny. We were called in to confiscate four Belgian draft horses from a home; the owners stopped feeding these guys months ago. They put them up for sale on Craigslist trying to get rid of them. The first family that stopped by to look at them immediately called the local animal control. We came and got them, and they need a soft place to land. Mind if we bring them to you?"

"Not at all, happy to help," smiled Jenny, she had no idea what she was in for.

Half an hour later Mary's truck turned into Jenny's drive, pulling a large trailer, with Paul's truck following closely behind.

Jenny helped Mary lower the trailer ramp, trying to go slow so as not to make too much noise, but when she saw the inhabitants, the shock opened her hands, letting the door clank to the ground. The loud sound startled the horses inside, their hooves scampering against the metal floor, one of them falling down. There was a battle of trying to get out, while trying not to tread on the already fallen horse near the tailgate. It was

71

already dead. The three horses still living were towards the front of the trailer, their eyes wide with terror. Whether it was fear of the unknown, or fear from the known horror humans had already done to them, no one could tell.

The dead horse on the metal floor was thin, too thin. It reminded Jenny of a set of dinosaur bones from the museum with the light sheet covering it, the front teeth sticking out, the dead eyes wide open.

Jenny looked away, the clanking of hooves against metal like fingernails on a chalkboard, the screams of fresh terror from the horses within. Paul went into action, first going into the trailer to try and calm the horses with his low voice. It helped a bit, until Jenny turned to look again at the scene and tried to stifle a scream by covering her mouth. The muffled noise was still loud enough to send the three horses into a frenzy.

The horses shifted into flight mode, the first one scampering towards the open door, nearly falling onto the dead horse, but able to jump clear and out onto the ground. Mary was able to catch the thin horse's halter while the others followed. Once all three of them were out safely, Mary and Jenny led them all to the barn, the two following the leader.

They came quietly, their eyes wildly watching for any sign of danger. They moved close to each other and did not want to be apart, so Mary opened one of the large stalls at the end of the barn, across from the twins. The three barely fit inside, but only because they were so emaciated. Two healthy horses would have a tough time moving around there.

All three wore halters, the smaller horse's halter was too small, even for how thin it was, and was scratching against the cheekbones, causing oozing sores. All of their hooves were all overgrown; they had lice, open sores, and dry crusty eyes.

Paul had come into the barn, still talking on his phone. "It's in the trailer, just stop on by when you can." He shut off the call, exchanging a knowing glance with Mary; she knew he was talking to Dan, the owner of the rendering company that helped with this sort of situation. "So, let's take a look at these guys," Paul said, trying to lighten the mood.

The three remaining horses were so thin, every rib could be counted. The back bones protruded so high they looked as if they were touched, the skin might burst revealing bone. They hung their heads low, searching for food. The youngest one was very weak, being held upright only by leaning against the other two.

Paul went into the stall and reached for the youngster; he wanted to remove the too-tight halter before it caused any more damage. The other horses crowded around it, protecting it from the intruder, but their weakness was no match for Paul's stubbornness. He gently held the halter, trying not to harm the little one any more than it already was, and pushed his way back to the stall door, pulling the colt behind him. He took him to the smaller stall directly next to the others; he was afraid the fear of separation might put them into more shock than they were already in.

The little colt was so weak he couldn't even lift his head. He staggered, then collapsed onto the dirt floor, which offered little comfort. Jenny rushed in, dropping to her knees beside him and gently cradling his head in her lap. In that instant, the caramel hue of his coat faded, shifting to a dull gray. The wooden walls around them turned ashen, and the bedding lost its warmth, becoming almost white as the color drained from the world around her. The colt lay still. Then, without warning, he stopped breathing. His eyes remained open—he hadn't even had the strength to close them. The shock had claimed him swiftly and silently.

The other two whinnied softly, as if to say good-bye. Mary gave Jenny a reassuring look, as if to say *it's for the best*. Paul walked out of the barn, making another call on his cell.

Mary went up to the hay loft and brought down 4 flakes of hay. As soon as they were thrown into their stall it was torn apart by the two horses, submerging their noses into the sweet-smelling heaven of their first taste of real food in months. Jenny filled the water buckets, knowing they needed fluids so they wouldn't colic from eating only hay.

Paul came back in with a small plastic container, throwing white powder all over the horses. "Don't touch them until the lice all die. I'll let you know when. I'll add their feed schedule to your chalk board, and I'll bring some baby food to help get some nutrients into them. So, until then, you'll need to feed them 6-8 times a day, in small batches. Give them only hay. We need to reintroduce food to them slowly. We don't need them to go into shock, well, more shock than they already are, and colic on us."

Mary, Paul and Jenny walked out of the barn, a quiet calm in the air. Paul had already closed the gate to the trailer, thankfully hiding the dead horse within.

About an hour later, a large flatbed truck loaded with a tractor rolled onto the property. Dan, the owner of the rendering company, stepped down from the cab and exchanged a few quiet words with Paul.

Paul then turned to Jenny. "Why don't you step inside for a bit?" he said gently. He gave a small nod to Mary, who immediately understood. Without saying much, she walked with Jenny inside the house, where they sat down for a cold drink in the kitchen.

Jenny, still shaken, asked softly, "What's going on?"

Mary gave a calm but honest answer. "Dan will be burying the two dead horses in the back of your pasture, by the trees." she said. "But the process of moving them… it's not always easy to witness. Horses are large animals, and unfortunately, they don't move easily once they're gone. Sometimes chains have to be used to drag and lift them onto the truck. It's not pretty, and definitely not something I think you should see."

Jenny nodded in understanding and didn't ask any more questions.

To change the mood in the room, Mary asked, "What are you going to name the two survivors?"

"Gabriel and Genevieve," Jenny quietly said, her head down as she sat down on the sofa.

"What's that?" Mary asked, following her.

"Gabriel and Genevieve," Jenny replied, picking her head up, turning to look at Mary. "Two angels I read about a while ago. I'll name them Gabriel and Genevieve," Jenny smiled for the first time after the horrible experience. "Gabe and Gen."

~ ~ * ~ ~

They were, it turns out, brother and sister. Large Belgian draft horses, the color of caramel, with light blond manes and tails, they were so skinny Jenny would have had no idea they were even draft horses except for their height. They were the first draft horses Jenny had ever seen, and their height was a bit intimidating for her, but their calm and kind demeanor quickly put her fears at rest.

They were very well-behaved: they weren't pushy around feeding time (unlike Yin and Yang); they came when they were called, they held their heads low to be haltered, and picked up their feet when asked. There was no reason why these two gorgeous creatures should have needed rescuing.

The next few days were critical. Jenny needed to make sure that Gabe and Gen got their food on the schedule prescribed by Paul, so she couldn't leave the farm. The rest of the horses were curious at first. *Who were the newcomers? Where did they come from? Why did they get to eat so much food? Why did they get lunch?* But after a day or two the novelty wore off.

Jenny did not let Gabe and Gen out in the pasture with the others yet. They needed sustenance, and calm, and the reassurance that everything was going to be OK.

"That's the crappy thing about this recession," Mary said, helping Jenny with the afternoon feeding one day. "Some people think of themselves before their animals. They figure the horse is so big, he can go without a meal, then its two meals, and before long…" Mary lifted up her hand and pointed at Gabe. She didn't need to finish the sentence.

After a week at Jenny's farm, these two gentle giants were comfortable enough with their new routine, and the new surroundings, that they were OK with being put in separate stalls, as long as they were still next to each other. Jenny was also able to separate the Yin and Yang into two of the smaller stalls, so the larger ones could be occupied by Gen and Gabe.

After three weeks of being cooped up in the barn, it was time to let them out into the pasture. Yin, Yang and Zaar Aza were out in the pasture for the day. Misha and Snookie were off somewhere playing. Jenny remembered seeing their tails bopping around the tall grass behind the house earlier, probably catching mice or voles. They were better than any pest control service one could hire!

After they finished their lunch, Mary and Jenny led Gabe and Gen outside. Earlier in the month, Paul had stopped by with a vet student from the University and put up a temporary fence right down the middle of the pasture, essentially chopping it in half. This way, new horses could get out without being shuffled directly into a herd. Everything with horses takes time, or so Jenny was learning.

With the manners that Gabe and Gen had already shown, there was no need for concern. There was no drama, it was as if they had been there all their lives. The other horses paid no attention to the two newbies.

Even Misha didn't notice the new horses when she did her morning rounds.

~ ~ * ~ ~

One week later, Jenny came into the barn to feed breakfast to the horses. She took notice that Gabe had not eaten his dinner and was lying down in his stall. She had never seen him lie down in his stall prior to this, and thought it was odd. When she approached the door to open it, he slowly got up and circled his stall, then he laid down again. Only, he wasn't just laying down, he was trying to roll over. Even though he and Gen were in the larger stalls because of their size, Jenny thought it was still dangerous to try and roll over in this small of a space.

She quickly called Paul to let him know of Gabe's behavior.

"Sounds like he's colicking, Jenny," Paul informed.

"Colicking"? What's that?" Jenny asked.

"Well, it's a general term for gastrointestinal issues. There are several reasons WHY a horse may colic, but the point is, he's probably got a blocked intestine. Has he pooped?" Paul asked.

Jenny looked around Gabe's stall and saw no manure piles. "No, nothing, not even any pee stains in the shavings." she informed.

"I'm on my way. Put a halter on him and start walking him around the pasture. He needs to stay up on his feet and walking."

Jenny tried her best to follow Paul's simple instructions. She was able to coax Gabe to stand up again and got the halter on easily. However, walking him around the pasture was not that simple. He kept lying down. The first time he did, she tried everything she could to get him to stand. Then she called Mary.

"Use the end of the rope and smack his butt with it," Mary instructed. "You've got to keep him moving. The movement may help loosen up whatever is blocking his intestines. If he lays down and rolls, he may twist his intestines, and that could kill him."

This panicked Jenny. She did not want another horse to die. Gabe and Gen had come from such hell, and they finally got out and got to a place with love and care. It would be such a pity to lose one of them now.

Jenny did her best to keep Gabe moving, and Gabe did his best to drop and roll as often as he could. When Paul finally arrived, Gabe must have rolled half a dozen times. Paul did his initial check, putting his stethoscope on Gabe's belly, listening for "gut sounds" as he explained. Nothing. Jenny felt like a failure once again.

For the next hour Paul did his exam and ended up giving Gabe some Banamine for the pain and then was able to get some liquids along with mineral oil into his belly by using a tube through his nose. It was painful for Jenny to watch, but she endured, standing next to Gabe, giving him as much care and attention as she could.

Once the medicine was in him, he settled down and no longer wanted to lay down and roll. Jenny was able to put all the other horses out to pasture, but Gen didn't want to go. She wanted to remain near Gabe for the day.

The next morning when Jenny went to feed breakfast, Gabe was in even worse shape. He was laying down in his stall, and there were circular grooves in the shavings that looked like he had struggled to get up several times but was unable to. She immediately called both Paul and Mary.

She fed the rest of the horses and let them all out, and again, Gen did not want to leave Gabe. His breathing was shallow, but very forced. Jenny could hear him breathing from anywhere in the barn. She also noticed that Gen didn't eat her breakfast and kept her head in a low position, as if she were grazing in her stall. Jenny began to worry. She was glad that Mary and Paul were on their way.

Gabe's breathing became labored even more so, so Jenny went into his stall and sat beside his head. She stroked his large, thin neck. He had only been there a month, and he was just starting to gain a bit of weight, but he was so emaciated to begin with, any amount of extra fat would not show up quickly. It took two weeks for the lice he came in with to clear up. It left his mane and tail a little stringy. But it was still a beautiful creamy yellow color, complementing the caramel color of his coat.

Gabe lifted his head, as if to try and get up, but then let it drop quickly, and heavily back to the floor. It hit with a loud thud! Gen stirred in her stall a bit but was quiet. Jenny tried to soothe Gabe, his breathing struggled even more so. The color began to bleed out of their world. Jenny watched his caramel coat as it turned to gray, his buttery cream mane to white, all the color was gone. Gabe took one last breath, and was still. Gen gave out a small nicker, and a hard kick to the wall, then fell to the floor of her stall.

Jenny quickly jumped up to see Gen lying in shavings, her head and legs thrashing about as if she were having a seizure. She watched Gen shake for about 45 seconds, then Gen lay still. There was no movement, Jenny couldn't even see Gen take a breath. Jenny felt so helpless. The color came flooding back to the world, and Gen's coat and mane reflected the same color as Gabe's.

She called Paul once more to give him an update. She knew he was on his way, and didn't want to bug him while driving, but things either just got really urgent or there was no need for him to rush after all. She let him make the decision.

When Paul arrived, he verified that both Gabe and Gen had passed on. "I'm so sorry, Jenny. I can't be sure what truly happened here unless I do a necropsy. Maybe the damage from the neglect was too severe. There's just no way to know."

Jenny knew she gave them a great last month of their lives. They were loved. They had plenty of food and water. They were clean. They had companionship. But she still felt like she failed them. She thought there was something she missed, something that she could have done better, or more of to get them healthier faster. There had to be something, and it nagged at her for weeks.

~ 9 ~
Galaxy

June, 2029

When Mary called and asked if Jenny had room for a particularly difficult case, Jenny hesitated. After what had happened with the last four horses—two dying shortly after arrival and Gabe and Gen passing just a month later—her heart was still raw. She wasn't sure she could handle another loss. But when Mary called, it meant another horse was in trouble, and Jenny knew she was needed.

Mary's description of the gelding's condition hinted at a nightmare: severe neglect, malnourishment, and multiple injuries. But nothing prepared Jenny for what she saw when he arrived. The horse had been abandoned by his owner and left alone in a cramped, makeshift, more a gravel pit than a shelter—littered with stones rather than bedding. There was no food, no water.

A blackberry bush had invaded the back of the enclosure, leaving the small space choked with thorns and barbs. A second horse had already died in the stall next to his. Volunteers from Animal Control had to cut through branches that had grown into the gelding's skin just to free him. The plastic water buckets were chewed down to jagged edges, likely from desperation.

Still, the heartbreak of the story didn't compare to the reality of seeing him in person. The gelding was skeletal—his ribs, hips, and spine painfully visible beneath a coat caked with filth and dried blood. His right eye was swollen shut, obviously infected, and he walked with a severe limp, barely bearing weight on his left hind leg. Covered in layers of mud, it was impossible to even tell what color he even was.

The Beechland Animal Shelter's vet had done a preliminary exam, but a full assessment was still needed. First, they had to clean him up. Jenny tied him to the wash rack and fetched warm, soapy water. The poor horse was terrified of the bucket, the sponge, the hose—every motion made him flinch. Even in his weakened state, he had some fight left in him. But Jenny and Mary were patient and gentle, and eventually he gave in.

As the warm water soaked into his coat, the gelding began to calm. He stood still, almost gratefully, while they worked. The runoff poured off him in thick, muddy streams—brown with dirt, blood, and who knew what else. As they washed away the grime, they discovered more wounds: embedded thorns, open sores, and infected scratches hidden beneath the filth. His ribs were even more pronounced once the mud was gone.

Jenny gently cleaned his neck, uncovering a patchwork of infected cuts. When they finally got to his injured leg, Mary understood the cause of his limp. A large stone was lodged so deep in his hoof that the split reached all the way up to the coronet band. The pain must have been unbearable.

Mary didn't wait for the weekly vet visit—she called Paul immediately. While they waited, she and Jenny took photos to document the severity of the gelding's condition.

When Paul arrived, he got to work right away. First, he examined the swollen eye and cleaned the wound. It looked like the horse had lost a fight with a rusty nail. There was hope he might retain his vision, but it was too soon to know for sure. Then he turned his attention to the hoof. The embedded stone required part of the hoof to be cut away just to reach it. Paul applied antibiotic salve, wrapped the hoof with vet wrap, then reinforced it with duct tape to keep it protected. The gelding was finally able to bear a little weight on the leg.

Paul examined the rest of his body, noting cuts in every area—including inside his mouth. Swollen gums had likely made eating painful, if not impossible. It was no wonder he was so emaciated. Hearing the full story, Paul concluded the horse had been trying to survive by eating the blackberry bushes, thorns and all. With each move in his tight, thorn-filled space, he'd injured himself further.

Once the medical evaluation was complete, they gave him a second, more thorough bath. As the last of the grime washed away, his true color was finally revealed: a sleek black coat dotted with dozens of tiny white spots. On his left shoulder, a faint, milky-white circle stood out—like a celestial mark, reminiscent of the Milky Way. Despite everything he'd endured, there was something quietly majestic about him.

Jenny gave him the name of Galaxy. It was her hope that by giving him a new name, it might bring good vibes to go along with his new life.

~ ~ * ~ ~

Mary needed to rush back to the facility and start the paperwork for Galaxy's case, so Paul decided to take the opportunity to do his weekly rounds.

"How about some coffee before you get started?" Jenny asked Paul as he headed for his truck.

He turned right around, winked and smiled at her. "That would be just about perfect. Thanks!"

He followed Jenny into her kitchen and sat at one of the stools at the counter.

"Why did you become a vet?" she asked him, just trying to make conversation.

"Have a while? It's a long story. But a good one, I promise."

Jenny smiled as she poured two cups, the rich smell billowing under her nose.

He said it was the path his life had always been on. Half Algonquian and, as he put it, half "mutt," Paul had been raised in the traditions of his Native heritage, embracing the stories passed down through generations of his family.

"This story's been told in my family for centuries," he began. "My grandmother used to tell it to me when I was little. Every time I heard it, she'd add more detail—more meaning—

like the story grew with me. Or maybe I was just finally old enough to understand it all."

He glanced at Jenny, then went on. "Apparently, I have a gift. An intuition with animals that runs through my grandmother's bloodline. According to her, every few hundred years, a set of twins is born in our family with this gift—one to heal, and the other to help animals pass on."

Jenny blinked, puzzled. "Help them… pass on?"

"To the other side," Paul clarified. "Cross the rainbow bridge." She nodded, understanding now.

"She told me I was the one born to heal. Convenient, I guess, for a vet," he added with a short laugh. "My dad thought it was all nonsense, though. He wanted me to take over his lumber supply company. Said all that spiritual stuff was just stories for dreamers. But I couldn't bring myself to work in an industry that bulldozes nature to put up concrete boxes."

Jenny tilted her head. "Wait… you said this gift appears in twins. So, you have a twin?"

He nodded, "HAD", his expression sobering. "A sister. But she died when we were three. I don't remember much about her."

He fell quiet for a moment, eyes distant. Jenny didn't press. She could only guess at the memories playing in his mind—his sister, his father, maybe both. She was about to ask whether his sister had ever shown signs of the gift when a soft scratching sound came from the glass door.

They turned to see Misha and Snookie perched on their haunches at the back sliding door, waiting to be let in. Jenny chuckled and opened the door. Snookie waddled straight to the counter, already on the hunt for her midday snack. Misha wound herself around their legs, purring and nudging for attention.

Paul watched Snookie's plump little belly jiggle with each step and smiled. "You've got her good and spoiled."

"Hopefully she won't meet the same fate as her mother." Jenny's voice dipped, the shadow of that terrible day creeping back. "Sometimes it feels like everything I care for ends up dying…"

"What?" Paul said, straightening. "If it weren't for you, that girl wouldn't have made it," he reminded her, pointing to Snookie.

Jenny shook her head. "No. *You* talked me through that. *You* are the one who keeps showing up to fix what I can't handle. Even that first day here—with the mare in the woods— it was you who helped the foals survive. Then Galaxy… Sometimes I wonder if I should even be doing this."

Paul leaned in slightly, his tone earnest. "Jenny, stop. You've got a gift—not like mine, but it's there. You connect with animals in a way most people never will. That matters."

Jenny wanted to ask him what his gift felt like. Perhaps even tell him about the colors going away for her, but just then, Snookie gave a loud chirp, impatient for more grapes. Jenny smiled faintly and crouched down to feed her. The room fell quiet, filled only by the soft crunching of Snookie's snack. Jenny didn't ask more questions, she sensed Paul wasn't finished with his story, but he'd share when he was ready.

When Snookie had eaten her fill, she padded back outside, Misha trailing behind her. Paul drained the last of his coffee and stood, offering her a small smile.

"Thanks for the Joe."

Jenny let him go about his rounds alone, her mind still lingering on everything he'd just shared.

~ ~ * ~ ~

Sadly, Galaxy didn't get any healthier right away. He had a very severe case of stall weaving that kept both his mind and body awake, never allowing him to sleep, and his constant whinnying during the night kept all the other horses awake as well. They couldn't wait for the morning when Jenny could let them out into the pasture, where they could get some much-needed rest.

Galaxy's stall weaving was particularly sad, weaving his head back and forth, back and forth, back and forth, moving his weight from one foot to the other. It was dizzying. "Horses tend to weave when stress takes over," Paul told her when she asked him what to do. Jenny just prayed that once he settled in, he would realize that he was in a safe place where he was being taken care of, and that he was no longer alone.

After being at Jenny's for one full week, Galaxy's appetite hadn't caught up yet either. His first meals were oats, which she watered down, warmed up and blended so as not to hurt his mouth any more than necessary. He was on the same feeding schedule as Gabe and Gen when they arrived, the same as any starved hose should get. She tried feeding him soaked beet pulp, along with some sweet Senior feed, but he wouldn't eat it. Day after day the buckets went untouched. She even tried soaking his hay, but it went completely untouched. He did drink water, but that was all. He was weak to begin with, but another week had come and gone since his rescue, and it seemed that everything she did to help didn't do anything at all. Jenny had decided that the next day she was going to call Paul in for some help. Maybe an IV would give him the nutrients or some medication he needed to jumpstart his system.

That night—Galaxy's eighth, something changed. His usual restless whinnying, which had echoed through the barn every night since he arrived, finally fell silent. For the first time in over a week, Jenny slept soundly. She even slept past sunrise, a rare luxury, noticing Misha wasn't there to serve as her usual furry alarm clock.

When Jenny finally made her way to the barn, the silence struck her immediately. There was no eager chorus of neighs, no impatient stomping for breakfast. Most noticeably, Galaxy wasn't calling out to her.

Concern crept in as she flipped on the lights.

All was still in his stall.

And then she saw it—a strange lump perched on Galaxy's back.

Jenny blinked.

It was Misha.

Curled up like a queen on a throne, the large cat was fast asleep on the gelding's broad rump, while Galaxy himself stood motionless, dozing with his head low and eyes shut. Jenny stared in disbelief. How had Misha even gotten up there? And why in the world had Galaxy *let* her stay?

But there they were, a picture of serenity and trust

Jenny held off cleaning Galaxy's stall, giving them both a little more time to enjoy whatever unspoken bond had formed between them. She went about feeding the others, all of whom remained unusually calm, as if respecting the stillness in the air.

Finally, she returned to Galaxy.

As she entered the stall, Galaxy stirred, his ears flicking forward as he slowly came to. The movement gently roused Misha, who stretched luxuriously atop his back before hopping gracefully to the ground. Without hesitation, she sauntered in front of Galaxy and rose onto her hind legs, front paws out like a begging bear.

Galaxy lowered his head toward her, gave a soft, huffing snort.

Misha licked his nose.

Then, as if that moment of connection was complete, she trotted out of the stall and out of the barn to begin her day.

Jenny stood frozen, stunned. If she hadn't seen it with her own eyes, she wouldn't have believed it.

From that day on, Galaxy's anxious stall weaving stopped.

And, for the first time since he arrived, he began to eat.

~ 10 ~
Journal of Virginia Dare
1603-1613

August 18, 1603

This day marks my sixteenth year, and my dear mother hath bestowed upon me this book, beseeching that I might record the chronicles of my life. I am Virginia Dare, daughter of Eleanor and Ananias Dare, and the first white child born in this New World.

I shall begin from the very start. As I have said, I was born in this strange and untamed land. When I was but three months old, my mother, father, and the others were journeying from one fort to another, when we were sorely beset by the Secotan, an Indian faction who opposed the settlement of our people upon their lands.

Many perished in that grievous attack, including my father. Oft I have wished to have known him, yet such wishes are but frivolous thoughts. My mother, Eleanor, hath raised me with care and courage. We now dwell among the Croatoan people. I shall continue to write in this journal as my days and adventures permit.

April 13, 1604
My dear mother hath fallen grievously ill. She took a fever these past weeks. Small red spots doth appear upon her skin, and no quantity of fresh water or medicine hath brought her relief. Several of the children have likewise fallen ill, many having passed from this world.
I remember well the council fashioning coffins for the little ones. They felled a great cypress tree and hollowed it as one would a canoe. The child was laid within, then covered with another hollowed piece, thus enclosing the body. Deep in the earth these coffins were buried. The day was one of great sorrow.

April 21, 1604
My mother hath passed unto the Lord this day. Being Christians, the Croatoan made for her a special coffin. Upon it was carved a Maltese cross and the letters "I N R I," signifying "Jesus Nazarenus, Rex Judaeorum." Before sealing the coffin, I placed within her diary, that her words might rest with her.
There remain but a few of the original white settlers living among the Croatoan, no more than fifteen souls. Many marriages have taken place between the white folk and the Croatoan, producing children fair of skin and

grey of eye. Now that my mother is gone, I find myself all alone.

June 9, 1604
This day I shall wed my friend Caratoke. My heart rejoiceth, for at last I shall have a family of my own.

September 25, 1605
This blessed day, I brought forth two healthy children, a boy and a girl. Both have eyes of blue, like unto mine own, and skin lighter than my husband's. We have named them Pocosin and Wysocking, meaning Land and Sea in my husband's tongue.

Winter, Anno Domini 1610
An elder of the Croatoan hath come to me bearing tidings of events past. There be two factions among the native peoples—the Croatoan and the Secotan. Before my mother and father came across the great ocean, earlier settlers dwelt here but found no peace with the Secotan. A stolen silver chalice brought discord; the Secotan were accused, and their leader was taken and cruelly burnt alive.
Thus the Secotan opposed further settlement, and did all in their power to drive us away. The Croatoan prayed earnestly for a sign from their God.
The elder told of a white buffalo that appeared upon the land, a wondrous sight sent to save us starving settlers.

The Croatoan deemed the buffalo sacred and warned against harming it. Yet the settlers, driven by hunger and pride, slew the buffalo. This act incensed the Secotan, who cast a curse upon the beast and upon those who consumed it, bringing sickness and death.

To prevent further harm, the Croatoan secretly took the buffalo and buried it in a hidden place. The elder shared a vision that only a sacred union between white and dark skins could heal the land and bring prosperity once more. He declared that my children were this union, though I understand not fully the ways of the Croatoan. Yet I deem this tale worthy of record.

Summer, 1611

My children grow swiftly and show great strength and kindness. An elder returned to tell me of the gift they share. 'Tis he who spoke before of the white buffalo and the healing union.

He tells me Pocosin hath a wondrous way with beasts. If an animal be hurt, it seeketh her, and she healeth it. I find it difficult to believe, yet the elder is steadfast in his faith.

Wysocking, he says, guideth those creatures who cannot remain in this world, helping them journey onward. Though such things seem magical to me, I cannot deny their wonder.

Autumn, 1611

If I had not witnessed it with mine own eyes, I would not have believed it. While walking with Pocosin among our horses, we spied a fox creeping through the tall grass. The fox gave chase, but was struck by a startled horse and fell lifeless.

Pocosin approached the fallen creature and sang softly the songs taught her by the elders. To my great astonishment, the fox revived and walked away, whole once more. Truly, this is a miracle.

Winter, Anno Domini 1613

The winter grows harsh, and my strength wanes. I have taken ill with the same grievous fever that so cruelly took my mother. Small red spots have appeared upon my skin, and my body is weak beyond measure. By the counsel of the Elders and for the safety of all, I am set apart in a humble tent, distant from the rest. My heart aches sore for my dear children, Pocosin and Wysocking, whose laughter and presence have been the light of my days. I pray fervently to God that He will restore my health, that I might see them grow into the fullness of their gifts and purpose.

~ 11 ~
Johnnie Walker

July, 2029

On a Saturday morning that summer, Mary called Jenny with another difficult case. Jenny was knee-deep in muck, cleaning stalls when her phone rang.

"Jenny, I know you're feeling overwhelmed, but this horse really needs you. He needs a safe place to rest and recover—and yours is the best place for that. Plus... there's a little bonus."

"What kind of bonus?" Jenny asked, curiosity piqued.

"A man! A man of your very OWN!" Mary teased with a laugh. "No, seriously. He's an actor prepping for a film involving horses. Wants to learn the ropes—barn work, animal care, the whole deal. Free labor. You can't say no to that."

Jenny groaned but smiled. "You're right, Mary. I need the help. When should I expect you?"

"Fifteen minutes."

"Perfect! Appreciate the heads-up!" Jenny said, rushing to wrap up chores and change. It being Saturday, that meant Kirsten and Linda weren't there for morning chores.

By the time she'd made herself presentable, she heard a commotion outside. Stepping out, she saw Mary and a man trying to unload a horse from the trailer. The horse was screaming and thrashing, hooves kicking wildly inside the metal box.

The horse eventually scrambled backward out of the trailer, and Jenny's breath caught. "Wow. He's beautiful."

"Thanks, but you don't need to be so obvious," a male voice joked from behind the trailer.

"I meant the horse," Jenny replied flatly, not even glancing at him.

"His name's BrandyWine," Mary said. "Champion Tennessee Walking Horse."

The tall sorrel gelding had a graceful build—long neck, sloped shoulders, pretty head with alert ears. His coat shone like it had been lacquered. Jenny was baffled; he looked healthy, not starved, and so very shiny he practically glowed. He didn't look neglected. But then she noticed his feet.

He wore unnatural, four-inch pads on his front hooves. His front legs were unnaturally close together, and his hind legs tucked far forward, making his entire frame resemble an inverted triangle. His agitation was obvious. He could barely stand still, but movement caused him even more pain.

"What are those?" Jenny pointed to the lifts. "And what's wrong with his legs?"

"That's why he's here," Mary replied, her expression heavy with sympathy. "He was subjected to soring—those pads are weighted and nailed into his hooves. The goal is to force a high-stepping gait. The cruelty behind it... it's heartbreaking. We need to get those off right away."

As they led BrandyWine toward the barn, he struggled, every step clearly excruciating. Jenny's heart ached.

Mary continued, "Sometimes those nails go too deep. That's what happened here."

"Why would anyone do that?" a deep voice came from the other side of the horse, inserting himself into the conversation.

Mary paused. "Oh—Jenny, this is Tristan Clay. Tristan, meet Jenny."

They shook hands. Jenny immediately recognized him. He was striking—too striking. Model-level good looks: high cheekbones, square jaw, green eyes that shone like spring grass. His face had the kind of polish that usually came with magazine covers, make-up artists and lighting crews. But his looks were all natural.

His rise to fame was the stuff of teenage dreams. Discovered in a mall at 14, he'd landed modeling gigs and soon transitioned into acting, becoming a daytime soap star. By 16, he'd won a Daytime Emmy. The success snowballed from there: more roles, more headlines, and eventually, a reputation for partying. But despite the scandals, he'd managed a comeback and now stood in Jenny's barn, supposedly doing "research."

"He's prepping for a role involving Tennessee Walkers," Mary added. "And I thought, given how full your barn is getting, you could use an extra set of hands."

"Thanks to you," Jenny said, half-smiling.

She was skeptical about the film story—Tristan was a rom-com regular, not known for serious roles. His personal life mirrored his screen career: a new girlfriend every few months, many of them co-stars.

Mary turned to Tristan. "Tennessee Walkers are known for their exaggerated gaits. The 'Big Lick' is an unnaturally high step, achieved through soring. Trainers use heavy pads or even caustic chemicals—gasoline, mustard oil—wrapped with plastic to inflict pain."

Tristan's eyes widened. "That's horrific. How do they get away with it?"

"They condition the horses not to show pain. Any flinch is punished. Before competitions, they let the visible wounds heal, making detection hard."

Mary crouched to touch BrandyWine's leg. "Feel this—hot and swollen from the chemicals."

Jenny shook her head. "No need. I believe you."

Tristan stepped forward to feel the legs, but as soon as he reached for the horse, BrandyWine panicked — rearing, snorting, eyes wide with terror. Tristan stumbled back, hands raised.

Mary calmed the gelding with soft whispers. "Don't worry. Paul's on his way. Removing those pads is delicate work. We need a vet. We don't know what we'll find under there."

Jenny watched BrandyWine, his beautiful coat and trembling legs, and felt the familiar swell of heartbreak and purpose. Another broken animal in need. Another soul to heal.

Forty-five minutes later, Paul's truck rumbled up to the barn. Without a word, he grabbed his tools and got to work. The first step was sedating BrandyWine—Paul needed him calm before touching his injured feet. As the medication began to take hold, Paul circled the horse slowly, humming softly, then slipping into a gentle song. The effect was almost magical. BrandyWine's trembling eased, his breathing slowed. Even the others watching seemed to relax.

"Alright, let's see what we're dealing with," Paul said quietly as he knelt beside the horse's front hooves.

Under each of the heavy pads, Paul uncovered metal screws—deliberately placed to dig into the tender sole. Worse still, the hooves had been trimmed down past the soul, leaving raw tender flesh in constant contact with the metal. It was cruelty in plain sight.

"Imagine cutting your toenails so short they bleed," Paul explained grimly. "Then shoving screws beneath them, soaking your feet in gasoline, and wrapping them in plastic wrap. That's what he's been living with. And that's just what we can see. Some trainers take them up and down concrete paths to worsen the pain—makes them lift their legs higher for the show."

As Paul removed the platform from each hoof, Mary snapped photos from every angle, carefully documenting the abuse. Every bit of evidence would strengthen their case against the owner in court.

Jenny's stomach churned. The thought that all this was done just to win a ribbon made her ill. But at least now, BrandyWine had a shot at peace.

"What happened to the owner?" Tristan asked.

Mary crossed her arms. "He's been banned from the show circuit—though that's hard to enforce. They tend to change their names, and the names of their barns, etc. Criminal charges are pending, but these things move slowly."

Paul moved on to examine BrandyWine's hind legs. They, too, showed signs of abuse, though not as severe. Thankfully, they should heal with time and care.

"Other than his legs, he's in surprisingly good shape," Paul said, gently brushing his hand along the horse's flank. "But the damage to his forelegs… it's the worst I've ever seen. He'll be sore for a long time, maybe for life. I've given him antibiotics to prevent infection and painkillers to ease his suffering. I also administered cortisone to reduce the swelling. That's all I can do for now. The rest is up to you—and him. He may lie down a lot to take pressure off his feet. Just keep an eye on him."

They thanked Paul as he packed up and headed to his next call. The others retreated to the house, quiet and thoughtful, trying to process everything they'd just witnessed—and figured out how best to help.

"I've got a pair of therapeutic boots back at the shelter," Mary offered. "Soft foam inside, like memory foam. They'll give him relief while he's standing. I'll bring them by tomorrow."

"I can grab them," Tristan said. "It will give me a chance to see the shelter and meet the rest of your crew."

"Sounds like a plan," Mary replied, smiling.

"I'll prep the stall," Jenny added. "Extra, extra shavings— make it soft as possible." It wasn't much, but she needed to do something, anything to ease his pain.

~ ~ * ~ ~

The next morning, Sunday, Tristan, driving a shiny black GMC Sierra, completely trimmed out with chrome all around arrived earlier than expected—so early, in fact, that Jenny hadn't even started the morning feeding. She decided it was the perfect opportunity to show him the ropes and maybe get to know him a little better.

Yin and Yang were already raising a ruckus, kicking their stall walls and clanging their empty grain buckets in protest.

"Knock it off!" Jenny called. "Don't make me turn this car around!"

She smirked to herself at the joke, amused despite the chaos. The twins finally quieted down, as if they knew they'd pushed just far enough. Jenny recalled the first time she'd tried separating them into different stalls—they had whinnied nonstop for half an hour until she returned, at which point they went suspiciously silent, pretending innocence. She had caved and put them back together, and they instantly calmed, almost as if saying, *"I missed you. Never leave me again."* Eventually, though, as they grew and the big drafts moved in, the twins were separated permanently, each taking a 12'x12' smaller stall of their own. Life had gotten much easier since then—for everyone.

"They make quite the pair, don't they?" Jenny said to Tristan, trying to spark a little conversation.

He chuckled but didn't respond, watching her closely, like he was still trying to figure her out—maybe wondering what drove her to this kind of life.

They began the morning chores by prepping one of the empty 14x16 stalls. Together, they laid down the very heavy rubber mats, poured out stall pellets, and spread fresh wood shavings. Yin and Yang looked on curiously from their stalls, while Johnnie Walker, formerly BrandyWine, remained indifferent to the bustle beside him. She could feel the less he moved, the better it was for him.

Zaar Aza stood calm and unaffected—steady as always. Galaxy, on the other hand, was clearly annoyed by the attention being diverted from him. He stomped and snorted as if to remind them he still had opinions. Misha, of course, had already dashed back to the house, so she wasn't there to calm him.

Jenny moved on to show Tristan the feed room. Inside were several labeled bins of feed and a shelf lined with supplements. Three dry erase boards hung on the wall; each one neatly filled with names and notes.

"This one's for grain and hay," she said, pointing. "That one lists supplements. And this one is for meds. Paul updates them every week after his check-ins."

Tristan stared at the boards. "Looks like a Wall Street ticker. Complicated stuff."

"Some days I feel like I have no idea what I'm doing," Jenny admitted with a laugh. "But Mary and Paul are amazing. I couldn't do it without them."

She began scooping grain into containers, carefully measuring out each horse's feed and adding supplements or meds as listed. Tristan watched quietly, taking it all in, strangely comfortable in the quiet routine. For once, he didn't feel the need to charm or entertain. Jenny wasn't asking for any of that—just help, and a little attention to detail.

After the feed was prepped, they climbed to the hayloft.

"We've got Timothy and Orchard Grass up here," she explained. "Each horse gets a different kind and amount depending on their weight and dietary needs."

She asked him to drop one bale of Timothy and two of Orchard Grass. He eagerly complied, glad to feel useful.

Back on the ground, he gave a quick sneeze as hay dust lingered in the air.

"You're not allergic to hay, are you?" Jenny asked with mock concern.

"Not that I know of," he replied, laughing. "That'd be a hell of a plot twist."

Just then, Yin and Yang resumed their commotion, eager for breakfast. Jenny handed Tristan a couple of grain buckets and showed him how to deliver the feed and hay to each stall. Then she grabbed a wheelbarrow, filled it with Orchard Grass, and led Tristan to the pasture.

"Six piles for five horses," she said. "One per horse, plus one extra. Keeps them from fighting."

They scattered the piles across the pasture, then returned to the barn to finish prepping Johnnie Walker's new stall. The soft mats and thick shavings were in place—now all that remained was moving him in.

The twins finished eating first and were let out to pasture, followed by Zaar Aza, then Galaxy.

Moving Johnnie proved more difficult than expected. He recoiled from Tristan immediately, his body tense, eyes wide, teeth bared. He was clearly afraid of men. Jenny, thinking quickly, used a carrot to coax his head low enough to slip a halter over his ears. It wasn't the most honest method, but until he was trained to lower his head for the halter, it worked.

Walking just six feet to his new stall looked agonizing for Johnnie. His steps were slow and delicate, his face tight with pain, like someone walking barefoot across broken glass. Jenny moved at his pace, patient and calm. As soon as they got him inside, he collapsed into the bedding with a deep groan, finally free of pressure on his hooves. Once he was down, Jenny put on the Cloud boots the came from the shelter. Johnnie didn't make as much of a fuss as Jenny thought he would.

Once done, Jenny and Tristan both exhaled in relief, their breaths syncing unintentionally. They glanced at each other—no words needed. If the moment had been less painful, they might have laughed.

Johnnie was now on full stall rest, while the others roamed the pasture. Jenny and Tristan stepped outside to watch them.

Yin and Yang darted playfully through the field, weaving between their elders like mischievous children. Zaar Aza stood in his usual spot, calm and removed. Galaxy munched peacefully alone. It gave Jenny a quiet satisfaction to see her herd content—healing, adapting, thriving. The barn finally felt like it was in balance. And with Tristan's help, the weight on her shoulders had lightened.

But the moment didn't last.

Zaar Aza, usually the picture of calm, suddenly wavered. Jenny watched in alarm as he dozed on his feet, then buckled, nearly crashing to the ground. He jerked awake just in time to catch himself, shaking his head. But it happened again—then again. Three more stumbles before he forced himself alert and shuffled to a new corner of the pasture.

"Is that normal?" Tristan asked, brow furrowed.

"No," Jenny said, her tone clipped. "Not that I know of. I'll ask Mary and Paul today."

They turned and headed back to the barn, the ease of the morning replaced with a ripple of worry.

"So, tell me Tristan," Jenny started. Jenny grabbed a fork and a wheelbarrow and started showing Tristan how to clean a stall. "Tell me something I don't already know about you!"

Tristan looked at Jenny for a moment, not sure if she already DID know everything and was putting him to the test or if she didn't really know who he was at all. He grabbed a fork of his own and followed Jenny pile for pile. "Well, grew up in Texas, but my Grandma and Grandpa lived in Alabama. I visited them every summer growing up. My Grandpa liked to act in Civil War Re-enactments during the summers. They attract a lot of vacationers. That's where I got the bug and became a Civil War buff."

"Wow. That's pretty cool! And true, not something I already knew about!" Jenny quipped. "Does it come in handy at all with your acting?" she asked.

"Only once I was old enough to be in the re-enactments myself!" Tristan replied.

~ ~ * ~ ~

The next morning, as Jenny walked toward the barn, she spotted Misha sprawled out on the patio in the sun. All four legs were in the air, her belly fully exposed to the warmth of the morning light. Jenny chuckled, and Misha turned her head lazily, giving her a single slow blink before resuming her sun-worshipping.

Snookie had more or less moved out months ago, off to live the wild life as raccoons are meant to do. Every now and then, Jenny would catch a glimpse of her—usually at dusk, slinking along the fence line or rustling through the garden. Sometimes, Snookie would slip back into the house through the small pet door Jenny had installed for Misha. She'd pad quietly into the kitchen, hopeful that someone might be there to offer her favorite treat: grapes.

When Jenny stepped into the barn, the scent of smoke stopped her cold.

Inside, Tristan was leaning against a stall door, a cigarette in hand.

"What the hell?!" she snapped. "Put that out!"

Startled, he dropped the cigarette and crushed it under his heel, grinding it into the dirt.

Jenny's voice rose even higher. "Are you insane? Do you know where you are? This is a barn, Tristan! Wood. Hay. Dust. You might as well be standing in a puddle of gasoline!"

Her face flushed with anger; she grabbed a water bucket from a nearby stall and doused the floor—making sure to soak his expensive leather boots in the process.

Tristan stared down at his feet in disgust, then shot her a look and stalked out of the barn, already pulling his phone from his pocket. Jenny could hear his raised voice outside, arguing with someone, probably his agent.

She had just finished refilling the bucket when he returned, his expression more subdued.

"I'm sorry," he said, standing in the doorway. "Not just for the cigarette—I know better. That was stupid." He hesitated, eyes flicking to the ground. "I guess it's time to come clean."

Jenny narrowed her eyes, tension still in her shoulders. "About what?"

"There's no movie. No role. There never was." He let out a breath. "I got a DUI—again. My agent pulled some strings, convinced the judge to let me serve community service hours. That's why I'm here."

Jenny crossed her arms, waiting.

"But…. what you're doing here—it's incredible. You've got something special here."

She eyed him for a moment, letting the silence stretch. It was true—having the extra help had made things easier, and Tristan had proven himself more useful than she'd expected. And—if she was being honest—he was definitely easy on the eyes. More than once she'd caught herself staring and had to snap herself out of it.

"I'm fine with that," she said at last. "But this is a volunteer gig. No one gets paid. Not even me."

Tristan grinned. "I think I'll survive without flipping burgers at McDonald's."

Jenny rolled her eyes but smiled despite herself. "Just no more cigarettes."

"Scout's honor," he said, raising a hand. "Although I was never a scout. I needed a good reason to quit anyway."

Jenny shook her head and turned back to her chores but couldn't help the small smile tugging at the corners of her mouth.

~ 12 ~
Shackleford Banks

August, 29 2029

It was late August—August 29th, to be exact—when Paul showed up unannounced early one morning, wearing his usual easy grin and holding out a fresh iced latte from Dannie's Diner.

Jenny narrowed her eyes playfully. "Okay… what's the catch?" she asked, taking the cup and swirling the straw to redistribute the melting ice. The summer heat was still clinging stubbornly to the season, already hitting 80 degrees before 9 a.m.

"No catch," Paul said, clearly lying. "Just a favor. Kimber's off on her honeymoon, newly married and blissfully unavailable, and I've got an annual checkup I can't do alone. I need a second set of hands. You in?"

Jenny considered sending Tristan in her place, but the idea of a new adventure was too tempting to pass up. Before she could talk herself out of it, she hopped into his truck. "Alright, let's go. But you're buying lunch."

As they pulled out, Jenny asked, "So, where exactly are we headed?"

"Ocracoke Island," Paul replied, gesturing toward the coast.

"Ocra-Coca-Cola-what-now?" Jenny laughed. "That sounds like a sketchy tropical vacation spot for drug lords."

Paul chuckled. "No cartels, I promise. Ocracoke is part of Shackleford Banks. It's where a herd of feral horses—called Banker Ponies—have lived for centuries. There are over 400 spread across the islands, but the group we're checking on lives on Shackleford Island specifically. About 120 to 130 of them. I volunteer every year to do their annual health checks."

Jenny raised an eyebrow. "Feral horses? On an island? How did they even get there?"

"There are a few theories," Paul said, settling into storytelling mode. "One goes back to the 1400s—Spanish explorers brought them over with Columbus. Others say English settlers in the 1500s brought them. There's a story about a ship called the *Tiger* that ran aground. The colonists had to unload livestock to keep the ship from sinking, so they tossed the horses overboard. They swam to shore and stayed."

"Seriously?" Jenny asked, intrigued despite herself.

"Yep. And then there's the Civil War story," Paul continued. "There was a massive battle in Virginia. Afterward, the surviving horses supposedly gathered at a 'magical' place. The ones healthy enough kept moving and ended up on the islands. The others... didn't make it. Legend says over 300 horses died and are buried somewhere near your place."

Jenny shivered. "That's a little too ghost-story for my taste. I won't be going grave-hunting anytime soon."

Paul smiled, letting the silence stretch for a beat before Jenny spoke again.

"Oh, by the way—I meant to ask. Zaar Aza did something strange the other day. He was out in the pasture, looked like he was dozing, and then he'd just... stumble. Almost fell over a few times. It was like he was drunk or something."

Paul's expression shifted to one of concern. "Sounds like sleep deprivation. Horses nap standing up, but they still need two to three hours of deep REM sleep every day. And they can only get that lying down."

"So... why wouldn't he lie down?" Jenny asked.

"Two main reasons," Paul said. "Either he doesn't feel safe enough to let his guard down, or he's in too much pain and is afraid he won't be able to get back up. My guess? A little of both. Galaxy's the herd leader now, so he may not feel like anyone's watching out for him anymore. And with his arthritis... yeah, lying down might seem risky."

Jenny frowned, absorbing the information.

"I'll add some Previcox to his meds when we get back," Paul said gently. "That should help with the arthritis and hopefully get him resting better."

Jenny nodded, grateful. "Thanks. He's such a gentle old soul. I hate the thought of him not feeling safe enough to sleep."

Paul just gave a small smile, eyes back on the road as they continued on toward the island—toward wild horses and a glimpse of history still galloping along the shores.

~ ~ * ~ ~

As the road twisted and wound its way closer to the coast, Jenny watched the landscape slowly transform—lush, tree-covered hills gave way to stretches of sand and scrub. The air smelled different here, saltier, wilder. Beside her, Paul kept the conversation flowing, sharing more of the local lore with an ease that made the miles melt away.

"This area is steeped in Native American history," he said. "The Algonquian tribes thrived here long before any settlers came. They were true horse people. The bond they shared with their animals ran deep—sacred, even. It's said each tribe member had a horse, but it wasn't a matter of ownership. The horse chose the rider. That connection was for life. If one died, the other never took on a new partner."

Jenny glanced at him, intrigued. "You're serious?"

He nodded. "Dead serious. There are even stories that when a rider passed away, their horse would wander into the wilderness and never be seen again—almost like it was mourning."

Jenny looked out at the open land, letting the story settle. Paul continued.

"The Algonquian were also known as healers. Some believed it was a spiritual gift; others whispered about black magic. Injured animals—wild ones, even—would find their way to their villages. And when they did, it's said they were healed, as if just being in the presence of the tribe restored them."

116

She raised an eyebrow. "That's... beautiful. Kind of eerie, too."

Paul gave a small smile. "There's always a balance, right? Light and shadow. Their land was also seen as sacred in another way—animals came there to die. Some tribes believed it was a chosen resting place, a final sanctuary. But others saw it differently. They thought the Algonquian were cursed, that death followed them. They steered clear of the territory, afraid the curse might spread."

"And the forest?" Jenny asked, noting the thick trees lining a stretch of road.

"Legend says the land gave back what it took. For every animal that died, a tree was born in its place—to restore the balance between life and death."

Jenny shivered slightly, not from the temperature, but from the quiet reverence in his voice.

"My grandmother used to tell me those stories every night," Paul added after a pause. "Her grandfather was an elder of the Croatoan people. Our family traces its roots back to that sacred lineage."

Jenny looked at him with new appreciation, sensing that beneath Paul's steady hands and veterinary calm was a deep connection to something older, quieter, and far more mysterious than she'd expected.

~ ~ * ~ ~

After two hours on the road, they finally arrived at the island and pulled into a small dirt lot overlooking the dunes. The ocean wind hit like a wall the moment Jenny opened the truck door, dropping the temperature by at least twenty degrees. She was suddenly grateful she'd thought to bring a coat, even though it had been sweltering back home. As she zipped it up and stepped out, her foot sank into a hidden hole in the sand, nearly sending her tumbling.

"You alright?" Paul called over the wind. "Watch for those. The horses dig shallow ponds to find fresh water—it's not easy living out here. Just mind your step."

Jenny steadied herself and took a moment to scan the area. Sure enough, the sand was riddled with shallow pits, some just a few inches deep, others more like small craters. Once she was sure of her footing, they followed a sand-covered road past the gate Paul had unlocked, which led into the protected wildlife zone—federally managed and off-limits to the public.

The beach unfolded before them like a quiet dream. The scent of salt clung thick in the air, and the fog rolled in heavy and low, casting the whole landscape in a muted gray light. The wind roared off the ocean, wild and relentless, making even conversation a challenge.

Paul scanned the dunes for movement, eyes sweeping the terrain. He checked for hoofprints in the sand and then began walking north. Jenny followed close behind, unsure what help she'd be. They trekked for about fifteen minutes before cresting a low hill—and then, just like that, the wild horses came into view.

A small herd stood barely fifteen feet away.

Jenny froze. Her breath caught in her throat, her eyes wide with disbelief. She nearly let out a gasp, but instead stood in stunned silence, struck by the raw beauty of the moment. The horses didn't bolt. They simply watched, calm and curious.

"They're protected," Paul said quietly, "so you can't approach them on public land. But out here, when they wander close to the preserve's edge in search of food or water, we sometimes get lucky."

The horses were small—between 13 and 15 hands—with broad foreheads, low-set tails, and no chestnuts on their hind legs. Their coats were shaggy and windswept, blending into the landscape like they were part of it.

As they moved a little closer, Paul began humming—a low, rhythmic melody that rose softly from deep in his chest. Jenny recognized the cadence as something ancient, almost ceremonial. The song seemed to have a calming effect. The horses perked their ears and slowly drifted toward him, unbothered, even drawn in.

"There's not much forage here," he explained, voice just above the wind. "They eat what they can find. Some winters, the Parks Department has to bring out hay or they wouldn't make it."

Jenny kept a respectful distance, watching as Paul worked. One by one, he moved among the horses, laying a hand on their flanks, their chests—checking for injuries, signs of illness. None resisted. It was like they knew him. The herd eventually closed in around him, and Jenny lost sight of Paul altogether, swallowed up in a sea of swaying manes and tails.

Then, a small red roan detached from the herd and made her way toward Jenny.

The mare moved with a slow, halting gait, her head hanging low, her legs stiff and uneven. Jenny didn't move, barely breathed, as the mare stepped right up to her and lowered her heavy head against Jenny's chest. Hot breath fogged over Jenny's boots, and instinctively she reached out, placing gentle hands along the mare's neck.

The mare was burning with fever.

Then, something shifted. The color drained from the world around them—the pink of the mare's nose, the golden sand, Jenny's own bright purple jacket—all faded into desaturated grays. Even the ocean turned a lifeless slate.

Jenny tried to call for Paul, but the wind swallowed her voice. The silence wasn't ghostly like before; it was grounded, deeply natural, like the earth itself was holding its breath.

The mare trembled, then slowly collapsed into Jenny's arms, pushing Jenny to the ground. Her coat was thick with a winter layer that hadn't shed, her bones sharp beneath her skin. Jenny stroked her gently, trying to comfort her through whatever pain she was in. The mare's breathing slowed... then stopped.

Jenny sat with her in silence.

It reminded her of Yin and Yang—of the grove, of the hushed stillness when something slips between worlds. This was different though—earthier, ancient.

Roughly twenty minutes later, Paul reappeared through the fog, eyes widening when he saw Jenny on the ground, cradling the mare's head in her lap. He knelt beside her.

"What happened?" he asked gently.

"She just came up to me," Jenny whispered, eyes fixed on the lifeless mare. "She laid her head on me… and then she was gone."

Paul laid a hand on the mare's neck. "She was one of the old ones," he said quietly. "I've been watching her for a while now. I guess she was ready to make the journey."

Jenny looked up at him and noticed, for the first time, that the color had returned—the green of Paul's jacket, the golden hues in the sand, the soft pink tint in the mare's muzzle.

She sat with the mare a few moments longer while Paul contacted the Parks Department. Someone would need to come out and tend to her remains.

But for now, they waited, two quiet figures in the fog, keeping vigil for a life passed, as the wind whispered across the dunes.

The drive home was quiet. Jenny stared out the window, her mind lingering on the mare that had died in her arms. It wasn't just today—it was a pattern she was starting to recognize. The red roan in the dunes, the mare in the grove, even the raccoon. And further back… it had happened before.

She thought of Rocky, her childhood dog. He had been her best friend, her protector. When he died, Jenny had been inconsolable. Trying to ease her pain, her Uncle Brian brought home three tiny kittens from the same shelter where they'd adopted Rocky. They had been abandoned by their mother, and Jenny, desperate to fill the void in her heart, threw herself into caring for them.

But within a day, the kittens stopped eating. The next, they could no longer lift their heads. They didn't meow anymore. They grew cold and still in her arms. Uncle Brian rushed them back to the shelter, hoping the staff could help. While he spoke with the vet tech, Jenny sat on the floor, cradling the kittens in her lap. One by one, they went silent—then limp.

It had been too much. She was just a child, but the grief felt ancient. In that moment, she decided she wouldn't get close to another animal again. Everything she loved seemed to die.

Now, years later, the feeling was returning—an echo she hadn't wanted to hear.

Paul hadn't said much on the drive either. There was a heaviness between them, an unspoken sadness neither knew how to name.

When they arrived back at Jenny's place, she invited him in for a drink, hoping to lift the mood. A couple of beers in, Paul seemed to ease up. Jenny took the opportunity to ask.

"You've been quiet. What's on your mind?"

He hesitated, eyes fixed on the bottle in his hand. Then, with a hollow chuckle, he said, "It's my birthday."

Jenny raised an eyebrow. "Sounds like a reason to celebrate—not mope around in silence."

Paul gave a tired smile. "Not when your birthday reminds you of the worst day of your life."

Jenny said nothing, sensing there was more.

"My sister died on our third birthday," he said, voice low. He closed his eyes, the weight of that memory folding into his posture. Jenny braced herself, unsure how to respond. She expected tears—but they didn't come.

Instead, Paul opened his eyes and caught her expression— her mouth slightly open, eyes wide with empathy—and let out a quiet laugh. "It's alright. Really. It was a long time ago. But sometimes… it still sneaks up on me."

He stood suddenly, the shift in energy abrupt. "I should go."

Before Jenny could say anything—before she could even wish him a happy birthday—he was already heading for the door.

She watched him go, the silence in the room settled around her like a memory she couldn't quite shake.

~ 13 ~
Journal of Wallis Twiford 1864

Summer, 1864

The ways of the pale faces are confusing. They fight fiercely with fire and steel, but for what? Not for land—the Great Spirit gave it to us all, but they have taken it all by force. Not for enemies—no others seek to challenge their power. Their battle is for chains on human souls. So many fall like leaves in the wind, so many spirits lost to grief.

We, the Algonquin, remain apart from this war, walking the old paths and honoring the land and all its creatures. I am thankful for this, yet the shadow of their conflict touches even us. My brother William and I have seen its mark.

One evening, sitting upon the hill behind our wigwam, the sky lit far away, more than twenty-five miles from our home. Flashes of fire like lightning struck from the soldiers' strongholds. The air smelled of burnt earth and sulfur, and through the quiet woods, we heard cries—of men, of horses, the sounds of suffering carried on the wind.

The next dawn, a sacred and sorrowful sight unfolded before us. Dozens of horses—some with wounds fresh and bleeding, some still burdened by the weight of their dead riders—came to the edge of our village, gathering beneath the birch grove where the spirits of the ancestors rest. Some trembled with weakness; others bowed their heads as if weary from their long journey.

William and I approached slowly, speaking softly with words of comfort learned from our elders. The horses did not flee. They seemed to know that we came with respect and healing hands. The smell of blood and death was heavy, the earth soaked with sacrifice. Their heads hung low, eyes deep with sorrow and pain.

We began the sacred task of freeing them. Saddles hung tight beneath their bellies, reins twisted and knotted around their legs like snares. Some had broken free and walked away toward the east, toward the water, the place of renewal. Others remained trapped in barbed wire fences—an evil man's trap—and we cut them free with sharp blades, tools given to us by the traders.

It took all day, but finally every horse was freed. We tended each one with care, washing wounds with cool water and wrapping them with cloth soaked in healing herbs—yarrow and sage, gifts from the earth. Some horses were too far gone. They sought only to lie beneath the birches and rest their spirits. I knelt beside each one, singing the old songs of peace and gratitude, stroking their manes and whispering prayers to the Great Spirit. I asked forgiveness for the suffering caused by the hands of man.

While I honored the fallen, William worked tirelessly to heal those still living. His hands steady and sure, he wrapped wounds and soothed pain with poultices made from willow bark and sweetgrass.

In the days and weeks to come, we buried the dead with ceremony—marking their resting places with birch bark and stones, calling upon the spirits to guide them on the journey to the next world. Those horses who healed were free to return to the wilds, walking east to the great waters, where the sun rises and new life begins.

Spring, 1865

When the snow melted and the earth warmed, William and I returned to the birch grove. It had grown in strength, the young trees reaching upward with bright leaves shimmering in the sunlight. The grove was a living prayer—proof that the land, like the spirits of the horses and men, was healing. We gave thanks to the Creator for this blessing, knowing that life continues in the balance of all things.

~ 14 ~
My Happy

September 2029

Jenny didn't change the gelding's name when he arrived. Maybe it was because he was so old, she didn't think a new name would matter much to him. Or maybe, in some quiet way, she felt the name still held hope—that he might finally get a chance to live up to it. Whatever the reason, Happy stayed Happy when he came to her barn.

He nearly stumbled, coming off the trailer. "He's blind," Mary said softly. "His owners gave him up. They didn't know how to care for a blind horse. And at 38, well… he's well past the age most horses live."

He was completely white, with a gray nose and pale pink skin visible beneath his thinning coat. But it was the curve of his swayback that shocked Jenny. It looked painful—unnatural.

He didn't move like he was in pain, though. His swayback had been caused by years of neglect: poor nutrition, an ill-fitting saddle, and a rider too heavy for him. The abuse had left him unrideable, which was likely the real reason his owners gave him up. He wasn't fun anymore. Jenny could only feel sorry for whatever horse had been brought in to replace him.

The worst part, though, was the saddle sore. It was the most severe Jenny had ever seen—a raw, oozing wound on his withers, where the saddle had ground into his skin without relief. The sore had never been allowed to heal.

"I'm just gonna flush this out a bit," Paul said, standing on the other side of Happy. It had become routine now—Mary brought a horse, and Paul showed up shortly after to assess and treat whatever injuries or issues had been neglected. "You might want to look away," he added with a teasing smile, but Jenny didn't. After everything she'd witnessed by now, she could handle it.

Paul pushed saline and an antibiotic cleanser into the open sore with a syringe, letting the infection drain. "I'll leave a small drain tube in place to help it heal," he explained, then gently bandaged the wound to protect it from flies and further irritation.

For the first week, Jenny kept Happy in his stall. The other horses reacted with varying degrees of curiosity. Yin and Yang barely noticed him, but Galaxy and Johnnie Walker were more intrigued. Happy was housed beside Zaar Aza, which made getting to know each other easier. Often, Jenny would walk into the barn and find one of their noses stretched across the stall partition, reaching for the other. Johnnie, on the other hand, was more agitated. He didn't like sharing attention—and Happy, blind and slow-moving, was another disruption in Johnnie's carefully guarded corner of Jenny's world.

After a week, Jenny knew it was time to give Happy some freedom. She couldn't bear the thought of living out a life inside a 12x12 stall, and she imagined he couldn't either. Horses were meant to graze, to roam, to belong to a herd.

Still, she was nervous. He was completely blind.

So she clipped a lead to his halter and walked him slowly around the pasture, guiding him along the fence line. He stopped often—sniffing the air, the ground, the fence—curious and cautious in equal measure. The walk took 45 minutes, but by the end, Jenny felt confident he wouldn't wander blindly into trouble.

Back at the gate, she turned him around and unclipped the lead. Happy paused, lifted his head to sniff the breeze, then walked forward on his own. After about 20 yards, he stopped and began to graze.

Jenny smiled, then opened the other stalls one by one.

Yin was first—lithe and energetic, she trotted toward Happy, gave him a cursory sniff, and then continued on to her favorite spot near the trees in the northwest corner of the pasture. Her short tail flicked as she reveled in her space, away from her brother for once.

Yang, true to form, charged out like a rocket, galloping one full loop around the pasture before settling in near Yin. He lunged in for a playful nip, but she was faster, giving him a warning kick—not to hurt, just to remind him of the rules.

Jenny turned her attention back to Happy.

Next came Johnnie Walker. His limp had improved dramatically, though he still flinched around unfamiliar men. He moved slowly toward Happy, sniffing him over like a dog sizing up a new pack member. Happy lifted his head in alarm and let out a sharp squeal. Startled, Johnnie backed off, giving him a wide berth before finding his own space in the pasture.

Galaxy went out slowly to the pasture, completely ignoring the new tenant.

Jenny hesitated before letting Zaar Aza out. If anything happened, she needed to be ready. Lead rope in hand, she stayed close to Happy as Zaar Aza stepped into the pasture.

To her relief, Zaar Aza didn't charge. He circled Happy slowly, assessing him, and then stopped in front of him. He let out a soft whinny.

Happy lifted his head and answered with a quiet nicker, as if to say, "Hello, new friend."

That was it. No posturing. No drama. Just a gentle connection.

From that moment on, they were inseparable. Jenny would glance out the window throughout the day and always see them grazing side by side. At first, they stayed close to the barn, venturing only a short distance into the field. But each day, as Happy grew more confident, they wandered farther—always together.

Jenny once read an article while waiting for her shift to start at a barn in Boston. The lounge was cozy and elegant, with overstuffed leather chairs, worn wooden tables, and piles of horse magazines scattered across every surface. Bored, she reached past the glossy equestrian covers and picked up a veterinary journal, flipping through the pages until something caught her eye.

It was a story about an old blind horse and his companion—a kind of "seeing-eye horse." The pair had been turned out in their pasture when a sudden snowstorm rolled in, heavy and blinding. But the owners weren't too worried. They'd braided a small bell into the seeing horse's mane. Each time the wind stirred, the bell would chime softly, giving the blind horse a sound to follow. This gave Jenny an idea, and she quickly ran through her house scavenging for a tiny bell to attach to Zaar Aza's mane.

The weeks passed like a well-rehearsed rhythm. The mornings grew cooler. Fog hugged the pasture until the sun burned it away, revealing golden light and red leaves scattered across the grass. Jenny would sit outside after lunch, watching the herd nap in the sun, their coats gleaming in the afternoon light.

Galaxy's limp was gone. His hoof had healed beautifully. Johnnie Walker moved more easily now too, and though he still kept his distance from most people, he'd come to trust Jenny, Paul, and after a long while even Tristan.

Yin and Yang finally felt secure enough to explore on their own, no longer needing to be in each other's shadows. And Happy… Happy had found a friend in Zaar Aza. The two elder horses stayed close, with Zaar Aza gently guiding Happy across the pasture. Jenny even saw Zaar Aza finally lying down to sleep again, something he hadn't done in a long while. Maybe it was the pain meds Paul had started him on, or maybe it was Happy's calming presence. Either way, he seemed at peace.

The farm—ranch, really—finally felt complete.

Six horses. Every stall full.

Six, her favorite number.

This, was her family.

~ ~ * ~ ~

A few days later, Jenny was sitting in her car, trying to get on with a task that she knew she needed to do, but had all the luster of something she hated to do: car shopping, or, truck shopping as it were.

Jenny knew at this point, she needed a truck. She needed one that could tow a trailer, didn't smell like wet dog (too much), and wouldn't leave her stranded on the side of the highway with a flat in the middle of a lightning storm. Her little convertible roadster just wasn't going to do that job. It was time to go truck shopping.

She eyed her phone like it might bite.

"Come on, just ask," she muttered, and sent the text before she could talk herself out of it.

Want to come truck shopping with me? I could use a second opinion. Also someone who knows what all the buttons do.

Tristan replied a minute later:

Only if I get to push the buttons. Also, I'm driving first. I call shotgun if we bring one home.

And that was how she ended up pulling into the dealership with Tristan Clay, international movie star and current barn helper, riding shotgun in her Mazda Miata with a travel mug full of Dannie's Diner coffee and a baseball cap pulled low.

"Do not let them sell me anything with leather seats," Jenny warned as they got out.

"Right. Horses and leather seats. Mud and cow poop. Got it," Tristan said, flashing her a grin. "You want durable. You want practical. You want—"

"Something I don't have to mortgage the barn for," she interrupted.

"Dream big," he said, and they walked onto the lot.

The sales guy spotted them instantly. To Jenny's relief, the man—Rick, according to his nametag—didn't recognize Tristan at first. He launched into his pitch about torque and towing capacity, pointing at shiny trucks with way too much chrome.

Jenny was mid-eye roll when it happened.

A kid, maybe eleven, skidded across the lot like he'd seen a ghost.

"Oh my gosh! Mom! MOM! That's him! That's Tristan Clay! From *Moon Chase*! That's totally him!"

Jenny blinked.

Rick blinked.

Tristan gave a sheepish little wave.

The kid started hyperventilating.

Five minutes later, the dealership had ground to a halt. Salesmen emerged from behind cubicles. The receptionist came out with a movie poster she'd somehow had stashed in a drawer.

Someone offered Tristan a donut. Jenny stood off to the side, half-amused, half-horrified, while her potential co-signer did autographs next to a used GMC Sierra.

"Are you kidding me?" she whispered when he finally rejoined her.

"What? I'm excellent at distracting people. Did you see Rick? He completely forgot to upsell you on the undercoating."

"Because you signed his daughter's shoe!"

"I sign what I'm given," he said with a shrug.

They did, eventually, test-drive a dusty blue truck with cloth seats, a clean engine, and not a whiff of pretension. It purred like a dream and handled the gravel test road like it was born on a farm. Jenny felt something she hadn't in a while: confidence.

As they stood at the counter filling out paperwork, Rick leaned in conspiratorially and asked Tristan for a selfie.

Tristan smiled. "Only if you throw in those all-weather floor mats she wants for free."

Rick hesitated. Then grinned.

"Deal."

Jenny gaped. "You just—bargained with a selfie?"

Tristan looked smug. "You'd be amazed what a little sparkle can do."

~ ~ * ~ ~

Jenny swore the new truck still had that "new car" smell—well, underneath the faint scent of hay and dog hair. The blue paint was no longer showroom shiny (thanks to one back pasture detour), but it was hers. And today, it was getting its next test: trailer shopping.

She eyed Tristan over the steering wheel. "You sure you're up for this?"

Tristan took a long sip of his gas station mocha and gave a solemn nod. "I have strong opinions about aesthetics, floor mats, and rear ramp clearance. I was born for this."

"Right," Jenny said, dry. "Because your resume includes 'trailering livestock.'"

"It also includes outrunning an explosion on horseback in *Desert Sun: Reckoning.* I'm clearly qualified."

Jenny rolled her eyes and turned onto the highway.

The trailer lot was a sea of shiny aluminum and glossy white fiberglass. Some looked like mobile horse palaces, complete with tack rooms and fancy ventilation systems. Others looked like oversized toasters on wheels.

"Why are there so many kinds?" Tristan whispered as they walked past a trailer with living quarters fancier than Jenny's house.

"Because horse people have Opinions," she said. "And horses have even more."

They were halfway through comparing slant-loads to straight-loads when it happened.

A guy in Wranglers and a dealership cap did a double take as they approached a gooseneck with a swing-out saddle rack.

"Wait a minute—are you *Tristan Clay?*"

Jenny groaned under her breath.

Tristan offered a sheepish smile. "Depends. Are you a fan or a critic?"

"Fan! My wife made me watch *Moon Chase* and now I'm hooked. You're the guy who jumps out of a helicopter on a mustang, right?"

"That's me. Though the mustang was a very cooperative Andalusian named Pepper."

In minutes, half the staff had wandered over. One brought out their teen daughter for a selfie. Another asked if he'd ever "ridden a horse for real." A third offered him a branded trailer hitch cover "just because."

Jenny leaned on the trailer hitch and muttered, "Next time, I'm bringing a mannequin."

Tristan leaned back next to her, sunglasses on, grinning. "You love it."

"I tolerate it," she said, but her smirk betrayed her.

Eventually, they narrowed it down to a solid 2-horse bumper pull with a roomy tack area and—crucially—rubber mats that didn't smell like a tire fire.

Tristan climbed into the trailer like he was stepping onto a soundstage. "It's got good acoustics. I could sing in here."

"Please don't." Jenny quipped

He ran a hand along the wall. "Smooth. Spacious. Feels like something Galaxy wouldn't file a complaint over."

Jenny nodded. "I'll bring him to test it, of course. If he gives me the side-eye, we walk."

Tristan laughed. "He's got standards."

"So do I. Mostly involving how many brain cells a horse trailer lets me keep."

They finalized the paperwork, and as Jenny signed the last page, the dealership manager handed her a branded travel mug and looked at Tristan like he might offer to star in a commercial.

"Free floor mats again?" Jenny teased as they walked out.

"Not this time," Tristan said. "But the mug's insulated. And the salesman said I could autograph his toolbox."

"Your signature is becoming currency."

"Someday it'll pay for your hay bill."

She grinned and tossed him the keys. "Drive us home, Mr. Hollywood."

He caught them mid-air. "Only if I can back it up to the barn in one try."

Jenny raised an eyebrow. "You hit the gate, you're buying the first load of alfalfa."

He slid into the driver's seat with exaggerated confidence. "Challenge accepted."

~ 15 ~
Coyote Ugly

September, 2029

It was early September, and the heat still clung to the days like a wet blanket. The only relief came when the wind shifted from the east, carrying the scent of saltwater and a cool breath of sea air. Jenny had just finished the evening feeding and was heading inside for a cold drink when she heard it—a strange and chilling mix of sounds from the barn.

A high-pitched scream collided with a low, guttural growl. The hair on her neck stood on end.

She ran.

Flinging open the big barn door, she was met with silence—but the lingering dust cloud near Galaxy's stall told her exactly where the chaos had happened. She approached cautiously, not wanting to startle anyone—or anything—that might still be on edge.

As the dust settled, the scene unfolded before her in broken fragments. Tufts of fur—black, silver, brown, and gray—floated through the air. Galaxy's right hind leg was streaked with blood from hock to hoof. Misha sat in front of him, her tiny body trembling, her head bowed as he gently licked her face.

Jenny's eyes scanned Misha's matted fur, spotting raw patches of skin, a shredded tail—bent at an unnatural angle, bloodied and limp. The black fur scattered around the stall had clearly come from her.

Then Jenny saw the crumpled form in the corner—a coyote, lifeless and covered in blood. The pieces fell into place. It must have picked up Misha's scent from the woods and chased her. In terror, she had run to the only safe place she knew: Galaxy's stall. She'd slipped through the small hole in the siding—her secret entrance. But the young coyote, small enough to fit through, had followed.

Galaxy had done what Misha had trusted him to do. He had protected her—and in doing so, had gotten hurt. She immediately called Paul.

Jenny reached for the lead rope hanging by the stall door and gently clipped it to Galaxy's halter. She opened the door slowly, murmuring soft reassurances. He stepped out without resistance, though he clearly favored his injured leg. The gash looked alarming at first glance, but once cleaned, it turned out to be superficial—a scrape, likely from the coyote's claws during the struggle.

After dressing the wound, she tied him to the crossties, giving him a soothing pat before turning back to the mess inside the stall.

The coyote's body lay still in the corner.

With a grim sigh, Jenny grabbed a tarp, wrapped the body, and carried it out behind the barn. She'd ask Tristan to bury it later.

Then she returned for Misha.

Jenny scooped the cat into her arms, wrapping her gently in a towel, careful to avoid the worst of her wounds. She placed her in the padded chair in the medical room, adjusting the towel around her fragile body.

Only then did Jenny return to finish cleaning the stall. Once it was fresh and dry again, she brought Galaxy back in, guiding him slowly and speaking softly.

Finally, she lifted Misha once more—cradling her with extra care—and started toward the house just as Paul pulled up.

Paul had always pretended to be indifferent to Misha— scolding her with mock irritation—but Jenny knew better. She'd seen him when he thought no one was watching, whispering to her and stroking her fur with quiet affection. So, the sound of screeching tires and crunching gravel didn't surprise her. Neither did the urgent shout as he came into the house.

He found them in the bathroom, sitting on the closed toilet lid, Misha cradled in her lap, wrapped in a blood-soaked towel. He knelt beside them, set his medical bag on the floor, and opened it without a word. Jenny hadn't been able to look too closely at the wounds—she'd waited for Paul.

They gently unwrapped her, revealing the damage. Misha didn't move. She was limp in Jenny's arms. Paul carefully lifted her onto the bathroom counter for a full assessment.

The bite wounds were deep, but clean. The most severe damage was to her tail—it was nearly severed, hanging by little more than fur and skin. Her ear was torn, split right down the middle.

"She's calm. No need to sedate," Paul muttered, more to himself than to Jenny. "Let's keep it that way."

They worked in silence, exchanging only brief glances as Paul shaved around each wound, cleaned them, and stitched where he could. The torn ear couldn't be mended. Misha would bear that scar. But the tail was the worst of all. Paul clipped away the hair holding it together. Misha only gave a faint glance back as it fell away.

Once he finished, he cleaned up, then gently lifted Misha in a clean towel and carried her to the living room. Sitting on the couch, he cradled her quietly, whispering the soft sounds Jenny had heard before—the ones he thought no one noticed. She left them alone for a moment and returned with a glass of iced tea.

Paul stood, laid Misha in her usual spot on the couch's armrest and headed back out to the barn without a word, leaving the tea untouched. Jenny followed.

He went straight to Galaxy and clipped him to the crossties. The horse stood with his injured leg lightly resting on the ground. Paul unwrapped the bandage and examined the wound. "He'll be fine," he said. "You did an excellent job cleaning him up!"

Jenny stood at the entrance of the stall, guilt creeping into her voice. "I should've patched that hole weeks ago. I knew it was there. I should've fixed it."

Paul turned to her, his tone firm. "If you *had* closed it, Misha would be dead right now."

As if on cue, Misha limped into the barn. She walked slowly to Galaxy, who lowered his head and gave her a soft snort of recognition. She rubbed her face against his legs, marking him with the scent glands in her cheeks, claiming him as hers.

Jenny unclipped Galaxy and let him walk freely back into his stall. Misha followed closely behind. When he settled in, she tried to climb onto the partition between stalls but struggled. Jenny gently lifted her and set her on his broad back Galaxy tossed his head once, then let her settle.

Jenny knew she wouldn't be moving anytime soon.

"She'll be alright here," Paul said quietly. "She's in good hands—or hooves, as it were."

Jenny rolled her eyes at the pun and smiled, tears still clinging to her lashes, as they walked out of the barn together.

~ ~ * ~ ~

One afternoon, Tristan showed up at the barn practically buzzing with excitement. Jenny was elbow-deep in mucking Yin's stall when he arrived, but she could tell right away something was different. His usual calm demeanor was replaced by a kind of boyish energy that made her pause.

"Sorry I'm late," he said, a bit breathless. "I was doing some research on the local area online last week, and a book I ordered finally came in. I got busy reading it and, lost track of time." He held up a thick hardcover book, the kind with old maps tucked inside and that distinct dusty smell. A paper scrap marked his place. "You're not going to believe what I found."

Jenny leaned on her pitchfork, cocking an eyebrow. "This better be good."

He flipped the book open, eyes gleaming. "There was a Civil War battle. Right here. Practically in your backyard."

Jenny tilted her head, intrigued despite herself. She knew Tristan was into Civil War history, but she hadn't realized how deep the obsession went. Apparently, there was a lot she still didn't know about him.

"It was the summer of 1864," Tristan began, reading from the page but adding his own flair to the words. "Union General David S. Hunter was retreating after tearing through Southern towns. His men were trying to escape Jubal Early's army and ended up fighting at Hanging Rock."

His voice dropped into that storyteller's rhythm, and Jenny, curious now, stopped what she was doing entirely. She stepped out of the stall and sank down onto a bale of hay, resting her chin on her hand.

"After the skirmish, Hunter's army pressed west, trying to get over the mountain near New Castle. But the terrain was brutal. The men were exhausted, starving. They began tossing aside everything—blankets, packs, even the loot they'd stolen from nearby towns—just to lighten the load."

Jenny found herself drawn in, the barn fading around her as Tristan continued.

"The next day, they tried to cross Potts Mountain on their way to West Virginia. But they hadn't realized how punishing the landscape would be. Horses and mules collapsed on the trail.

Starving, too weak to go on. They had to be killed where they fell."

Tristan looked up, his expression solemn. "The locals buried between 250 and 300 animals. And they had to burn about fifty wagons—there were no horses left to pull them."

Jenny blinked, surprised by how moved she was. "That's… intense."

"I know, right?" Tristan said, lighting up again. "And it happened just a few miles from here. Can you imagine what's still out there? Old buckles, buttons, bits of harness—anything. I'd love to go scavenging sometime, see what history's been left behind."

Jenny shook her head, grinning. "Give you a bloody war and some buried relics and you light up like a kid at Christmas."

He laughed, not the least bit embarrassed. "What can I say? History's alive out there—you just have to know where to dig."

~ 16 ~
Katrina
August 29, 2005

"Damn it! I had fishing plans this week! Can't we send someone else?"

Brian Ritter, co-owner of Ritter Brothers Construction, wasn't typically the one making sales calls. That was Josh Coleman's job—Vice President of Estimating and resident smooth talker. But Josh had been rushed to the ER the night before with a severe case of kidney stones, and that left Brian scrambling to cover his trip to New Orleans.

"You're acting like a petulant child," Brenda snapped. "Just take the ticket and get going."

She was right. An emergency was an emergency, and Brian was the only one left to handle it. The meeting was with Paul Payne, Sr., owner of Payne Lumber, and Brenda had already confirmed the appointment. She'd even gone so far as to book a table at GW Fins in the French Quarter—Brian's favorite seafood spot. After rearranging his week on short notice, she figured he'd appreciate a little comfort food. Brenda was nothing if not meticulous. She knew Brian's schedule better than he did, and probably knew him better too.

Paul Payne, Sr., showed up right on time. They ordered drinks—technically not against company policy, though generally frowned upon. But hey, this was New Orleans.

Storm warnings were already in effect. It was late August—peak hurricane season—and the skies were threatening. Still, Brian figured he'd wrap things up quickly and get out before the weather turned.

"So, what happened with Josh?" Paul asked, sipping his beer.

"Kidney stones. Nasty business," Brian replied, wincing as he scanned the menu.

"Really? He seems too young for that."

They made small talk as the storm gathered outside. Paul offered a 10% discount if Ritter Brothers agreed to pre-order all lumber packages with a three-week lead time. Brian countered with 15%. The deal came together quickly—too easily, in fact. Josh had clearly done most of the legwork already. All Brian had to do was show up, schmooze a little, and sign on the dotted line. For once, he didn't mind being the closer.

As they finished their drinks, a sudden gust of wind tore one of the patio umbrellas from its base. It crashed into a nearby storefront with a deafening thud, spiderwebbing the glass. The restaurant fell silent, every patron staring wide-eyed at the damage.

Taking the not-so-subtle cue, Brian and Paul wrapped things up. Contracts signed, hands shaken, they stepped out into the chaos. The wind howled harder now, flipping their umbrellas inside out and sending them tumbling across the street like discarded toys.

They parted ways—Paul headed for his hotel to collect his family before rushing to the airport, determined to get them out before things got worse. Brian returned to his bed-and-breakfast, already booked under Josh's name. No point trying to find a new place at the last-minute.

By the time Brian arrived, the storm had a name: Katrina. She had been upgraded to a Category 5 hurricane and was barreling straight toward New Orleans. Officials issued immediate evacuation orders—but it was too late. The airport was closed. No flights in or out.

With nowhere else to go, Brian hunkered down at the B&B, ready to ride it out.

Megan and Morgan, the owners, had already boarded up the windows and hauled all outdoor furniture inside. They were just back from a final supply run—candles, batteries, water, and flashlights in tow. Brian pitched in where he could, helping secure the property.

When everything was done, the three of them retreated indoors, bracing for whatever came next.

All through the night and into the next day, the lights flickered sporadically as relentless rain soaked the streets. The wind pounded so fiercely at times it sounded like a jet engine roaring overhead. A sudden crash shattered one of the windows when a piece of debris hurled through the storm with a sharp, screaming whistle. Eventually, the power gave out completely. Huddled in the kitchen, Megan, Morgan, Brian, and another stranded couple gathered around flickering candlelight, waiting for daylight to try and get the generator running.

When the storm finally calmed, Brian began to feel claustrophobic. Trapped inside with the B&B owners and one other couple—all vacationers stranded by the hurricane—he longed to see the world beyond the walls. Curiosity pushed him to take a quick drive, just to survey the damage.

The storm had triggered a massive exodus from the city—planes, trains, and cars flooding every route out. Brian felt oddly grateful for the car rental mix-up that left him behind the wheel of an ostentatious Hummer instead of his usual sedan. The vehicle's high clearance was a blessing in the rising floodwaters. With the window down and the radio off, Brian soaked in the devastating sights.

Despite news reports claiming the damage was unprecedented, Brian was unprepared for what he saw. The city's main levee had broken, sending water cascading through miles of neighborhoods. Everywhere he looked, homes were submerged or shattered. Debris littered every street. People were stranded—some trapped in their homes, others clinging to rooftops, many separated from loved ones. The chaos was overwhelming.

As Brian passed an alley, a faint whining caught his attention. He pulled the Hummer to a stop and listened. The soft whimpering came again—at first, he thought it was a small dog. But as he scanned the area, he realized it was a little girl. Clutching a fire escape ladder on the side of a building, water rising several feet below her, she was drenched, terrified, and alone.

Without hesitation, Brian parked in two feet of water and waded through the flood to her. Calmly, he reassured her, telling her not to be afraid. She clung to him as they waded their slow way back to the truck.

The girl looked about three years old, but shock had clouded her memory. When Brian asked her name, she trembled and whispered, "J… J… Jen…nnn…nnn…ee."

Brian knew the odds of finding her family amid such chaos were slim, but he vowed to do everything he could to reunite this frightened child with her loved ones. He had no idea this promise would shape the rest of his life.

Back at the B&B, Brian helped get her cleaned up and warm. Poor Jenny barely let go of him, so frightened was she. Megan did her best to soothe the girl as she clung tightly to Brian. After a warm bowl of soup and a cozy blanket, Jenny finally drifted into a deep, peaceful sleep.

She slept through the day and night, unfazed even by the howling wind, heavy rain, and another power outage—like a fragile doll in a storm.

The next morning, Brian set out for the Astrodome, where most displaced families had been evacuated. He hoped to find Jenny's family there.

Inside the massive arena, tables stretched in neat rows for families to check in and register missing persons. The scene resembled a refugee camp in a war-torn country—crowds waiting in lines that stretched 40 deep at each of the 25 stations. The buzz inside was constant and overwhelming, like the hum of a hive, loud and unceasing.

It took Brian 45 minutes to get through the first line, only to learn it was for checking in evacuees—not for reporting missing persons. Undeterred, he switched to the line for lost and found, holding onto hope that "Jenny" might be enough to find her family.

Most people in the dome were African American and from lower-income neighborhoods; Brian spotted only a few white families. When he asked them about Jenny, they all shook their heads, apologetic but not her family.

Finally, Brian noticed a woman standing by the list of missing children. Her eyes were red-rimmed, her face swollen from crying.

"Excuse me," Brian said softly, stepping closer and gently touching her shoulder. She turned, weary but alert.

"Yes? What can I do for you?" she asked.

"I'm looking for a family," Brian began.

"Who isn't?" she replied tiredly.

"No, I mean a little girl. I found her during the storm, and I want to find her family."

Her eyes brightened, glistening with tears. "I'm looking for my daughter," she said desperately. "Her name is Virginia."

Brian's heart sank. "I'm so sorry. She isn't your daughter."

Tears spilled down her cheeks, but she managed a grateful smile. "Thank you. Thank you for looking. I pray you find her family."

Brian was stunned by her grace and kindness, touched that she would offer prayers for him despite her own heartbreak.

"I pray you find your daughter, too," he said quietly, squeezing her shoulder.

They parted ways—both weighed down by disappointment but buoyed by hope that somewhere in the sea of faces, their missing loved ones would be found.

~ ~ * ~ ~

(6 months earlier…)

"Pregnant? *Pregnant?* Are you kidding me?" Pete Ritter's voice thundered through the office. "How the hell could you let this happen, Brian?"

Brian leaned back in his chair, unfazed. "Well, you know… when two people really like each other—"

"Don't joke with me right now," Pete snapped. "I'm sick of cleaning up after your messes. Jesus, Brian. How old is she this time?"

Brian sighed. "Eighteen. I think. Relax, Pete—it's handled. Just like last time."

Pete's eyes widened in disbelief. "Handled? You keep saying that, like it erases the disaster behind it. And don't pretend you don't know what messes I'm talking about. Want

155

me to start with the $250 you tried to expense for coffee at Java Jugs?"

Brian smirked. "You should see what they put in their espressos. Pretty unforgettable."

"You're unbelievable. Just because you made a fortune betting on horses and got out lucky doesn't mean you know a damn thing about real responsibility. We're partners now, or did you forget that?"

Brian didn't answer immediately. He tugged at the cuff of his worn Carhartt jacket, his eyes fixed on the fraying button. "We *are* in this together. George took care of it. It's done."

Then, as if to punctuate his indifference, Brian lit a cigarette. Pete grimaced—he hated smoking. Their offices were tucked in the back of the building, side by side, separated by a sliding glass window for convenience. Pete slammed it shut with a bang, and a sharp crack split down the center of the glass—perfectly straight, clean.

Brian stared at it for a long moment.

Two halves.

Without another word, he stubbed out his cigarette, grabbed his keys, and walked out. It was quitting time anyway.

Pete followed not long after, the tension still boiling under his skin.

By the time Brian pulled into his garage, the sun had dipped below the horizon. He killed the engine, slouched in his seat, and his phone buzzed. It was Pete.

"Yeah?" Brian answered flatly.

"I'm sorry," Pete said with a sigh. "You frustrate the hell out of me. I know I come down hard on you. It's just—Hi, honey."

Brian blinked. "What?"

"I just walked in the door," Pete added, distracted. "I'll call you later."

Brian was about to hang up when he heard Pete's voice again, muffled. Pete hadn't ended the call—just shoved the phone in his pocket.

"You'll never guess what Brian did this time," Pete told his wife.

Brian's finger hovered over the hang-up button.

"What now?" Anna asked.

"He got another girl pregnant. And George handled it, like before."

There was a long silence. Then Anna's voice, quiet and breaking: "I can't believe it. He didn't learn the last time? After everything we've been through? Pete… we've been trying for *so long*…"

Brian sat frozen, unable to tear himself away.

"We can't even adopt," Anna continued, her voice cracking. "My health... the agency turned us down. And he just—he just throws it away like it's nothing."

Her sobs began softly, painfully, echoing through Brian's speaker.

Guilt twisted in his gut. He finally ended the call, but the damage was done. He felt like he'd cracked open a door he was never meant to touch.

He sat in the silence of his garage, staring at nothing, then finally stepped out of the car and went inside, each step heavier than the last.

~ ~ * ~ ~

Pete and Anna's conversation continued in the soft light of the kitchen, her back to him as she stirred something on the stove.

"Anna, he doesn't know. You can't hold this against him," Pete said quietly. "He's just being Brian. Doing what he's always done."

She turned sharply. "And you're doing what *you've* always done—covering for him. Picking up the mess so he never has to look at the damage." Her voice cracked, not from anger, but exhaustion. "I get it, Pete. He's your brother. But when is enough finally enough?"

Pete didn't answer. He leaned against the counter, arms folded tightly across his chest.

Anna threw the dishtowel down. "I know his moral compass has always been... off. I swear, he thinks 'morals' are just wall décor and 'scruples' is some kind of Russian currency. But two pregnancies? Two? And he just sweeps it under the rug?"

She paused, breathing hard, her eyes wet again. Then, more softly: "What are we even doing, Pete?"

The room fell silent except for the low simmer of something on the stove.

Sometimes, Anna couldn't believe they were even from the same bloodline. If it weren't for the unmistakable family resemblance—those freckled cheeks, that stubborn red hair, and the same crooked Irish grin—she might have questioned if Brian had been switched at birth. But it was more than appearance. They shared that same goofy, irreverent humor, that uncanny ability to charm a room. And Brian had it in spades.

His face was more angular, almost roguishly handsome. Despite being five years older, he carried himself with an effortless confidence. Women didn't just fall for him—they flocked to him. Add that to the money he made at the track, and Brian was practically a walking magnet. George, his accountant and longtime friend, had followed every bet Brian made. And it paid off—handsomely.

But that was only one side of him.

There were nights when the brothers would go out and, for a few hours, become the very best versions of themselves. They'd invite strangers to their table like old friends. Share stories that had everyone leaning in and laughing until their sides hurt. Pete and Brian, in sync, storytelling like it was an art. In those moments, Anna couldn't help but love Brian—truly love him—not just as her husband's brother, but as part of her own family.

She sat down heavily at the kitchen table, rubbing her eyes.

"I don't know why I'm crying," she whispered. "It's not like I'm surprised."

Pete knelt beside her and took her hand gently.

"I know it's unfair," he said. "And I know how much it hurts. I just… I can't hate him, Anna. I want to sometimes, but I can't."

She nodded, eyes fixed on the middle distance. "I don't hate him either. That's what makes this worse."

She reached for a napkin, wiped her cheeks, then stood and straightened her shoulders.

"It doesn't matter now," she said, more firmly this time. "Let's just eat before everything gets cold."

Pete watched her for a moment, then turned to grab the plates.

The silence that followed wasn't empty—it was full of things neither of them were ready to say.

~ 17 ~
Riven Coffins

October, 2029

After an unusually hot and parched summer, the arrival of rain felt like a long-awaited reprieve. Cool droplets fell steadily, rinsing the film of dust from Jenny's old pickup, softening the sunbaked earth, and reviving the browning fields. The thirsty ground at first resisted, pooling water in wide, shallow lakes across the pasture before finally beginning to absorb it. The once-cracked soil now turned to mud, slick and deep in places, making any crossing without boots a messy gamble.

Even the horses, who had delighted in rolling across the dampened grass in the early days of rain, began avoiding the deeper puddles, leaping over them as if wary of being swallowed whole. What started as playful romping turned cautious, almost superstitious.

At the far northwest corner of the property, a curious rise stood out—an odd, square mound about thirty feet across and six feet high. Jenny had noticed it before, but with the return of the rain, she paid more attention to it. One morning, she spotted Yin and Yang frolicking atop the knoll, clearly preferring its drier ground. At the time, she assumed they just wanted to avoid the mud.

But then something changed.

About a week into the rains, Jenny noticed something protruding from the side of the mound—dark, jagged shapes emerging through the softening earth. At first, she thought they were logs or perhaps remnants of an old tree root system. But they were too uniform. Too deliberate.

Curiosity piqued and concern rising—especially for the safety of the foals—Jenny decided not to investigate alone. She waited for Tristan, knowing he'd be eager for a mystery, especially one involving mud and old secrets.

Together, they slogged across the soggy pasture, boots sinking and squelching with each step. The foals trailed behind, curious but cautious. As they reached the mound, the truth became impossible to deny.

Coffins.

Five of them.

Jenny stared, her mouth slightly open. "Is this… a cemetery?"

Tristan didn't answer at first. His eyes scanned the scene, drawn to the shapes and angles poking through the ground—three large, two small. The adult-sized coffins were modestly carved, plain and utilitarian. Child-sized ones lay askew nearby, half-emerged from the earth like forgotten relics.

The wood was old, rough-hewn, and darkened with age and moisture. These weren't modern caskets. They looked handmade, carved from split logs hollowed out to hold a body. Primitive. Intimate. Sacred.

Two of the adult coffins had come open—likely disturbed by the curious hooves of the foals. Jenny and Tristan cautiously peered inside. Only bones remained, carefully laid out and undisturbed save for time's weathering hand. A small, carved wooden block served as a headrest.

In each open coffin, tucked beside the skeletal remains, sat a leather-bound book—old, water-damaged, but unmistakably a journal. The parchment pages were swollen and warped, ink bleeding across the fibers.

Jenny knelt beside one, carefully picking it up. "These need to be preserved," she murmured. "There might be names. Stories."

Each lid bore a carved cross, simple and deep. Beneath it, four letters had been chiseled into the wood: **I N R I**.

Tristan broke the silence, his voice low. "I did a period piece once—colonial America. They used that inscription a lot back then. It's Latin: *Iesus Nazarenus, Rex Iudaeorum*. Jesus of Nazareth, King of the Jews."

Jenny looked up at him. "So… they were Christian?"

"Definitely," he nodded. "Probably early settlers. This mound might've been a private burial site, long forgotten."

Jenny swallowed hard. What they'd found wasn't just curious—it was historic. Sacred.

"I need to call someone," she said finally. "These coffins need to be reburied. Properly. Respectfully." She glanced toward the pasture. "There's no way you and I, and a couple of shovels, can handle this."

Tristan gave a half-smile. "I'm not afraid of mud, but yeah... we'll need more than elbow grease."

"I'll call Paul," Jenny said as they turned back toward the barn. "He knows the guy who helps him bury horses. I'll get the number."

Behind them, the foals danced along the edges of the mound, unaware of the weight of history that had just risen to the surface.

~ ~ * ~ ~

"I'll get a temporary fence put up to keep the horses out," Tristan said, as Jenny rambled off into the house. Back inside the house, Jenny made her way to the living room, the old books cradled carefully in her arms. Her hands were still damp from the rain-soaked pasture, but she didn't care. Her mind was buzzing with curiosity. She set the journals gently on the coffee table, then walked over to the fireplace.

With a flick of a switch, the gas flames roared to life, casting a warm orange glow across the room. It was the first time she'd used the fireplace since moving in, and the timing couldn't have felt more perfect. The crackling fire added a certain weight to the moment—like lighting a candle before diving into a long-forgotten ritual.

She curled up on the couch, pulling a throw blanket over her lap, then reached for the first journal. The leather was soft and worn, supple with age. She ran her fingers along the spine, feeling the imperfections, the years etched into every crease and fold. A faint, earthy smell drifted up—dust, parchment, and time itself. There was the barest hint of mildew, and she silently hoped the rain hadn't done more damage than she could see.

Carefully, she opened the cover. The first page had yellowed but was intact. In the neat, looping script of another century, it read:

Journal of Eleanor Dare, 1587

Jenny dove in immediately, her fingers carefully parting the delicate pages. The name on the first surviving page struck a chord—**Eleanor Dare**. That rang a bell from long-ago history classes. She'd been someone important... maybe came over on the Mayflower? Or was it Jamestown?

Growing up in Boston, Jenny had been surrounded by colonial lore—Paul Revere's house, cobblestone streets, Revolutionary War reenactments. But history had never been her thing. She was more of a number's girl. Math made sense. History felt like a messy puzzle with too many missing pieces.

Still, the mystery unfolding in her hands had her hooked.

Unfortunately, the journal hadn't fared well in the elements. Many of the early pages were warped together, waterlogged and unreadable. Others were little more than crumbling fragments. But scattered throughout the first section, a few passages remained legible—enough to piece together a glimpse of a life long past.

The journal began:

The 6th Day of Februarie, in the Yeare of our Lord 1587
This day my Father, Master John White, did come unto
me with most wondrous and joyful news: Her Majestie
the Queen hath named him Governour of the first
English Colonie to be planted in the New World. The
charge is great, and the honour greater still. Preparations
are already in motion, and we are to set forth within a
fortnight. My heart is full of marvel and anticipation—for
what greater adventure might there be than to cross the
vast Ocean Sea and begin a new life upon a land
unknown?

The 22th Day of Julie, 1587
At long last we have made landfall, our ships anchoring
near the place called Roanoak. The voyage was long and
sore, the latter days most grievous unto me, for I was
heavy with child and longed to stand again upon
xxxxxxxxxxxxxxxxxxxxxxxxxxxxxxxxxxxx
xxxxxxxxxxxxxxxxxxxxxxxxxxxxxxxxxxxxxxxxxxxxxxxxxxx
xxxxxxxxxxxxxxx bites cruelly.

Straightaway we began to unship our victuals and
goods, setting to work to fetch water and timber. We had
hoped to find fifteene men left from a former voyage, yet
found naught but bones. 'Twas a grim welcome.

Manteo, a native man of the Croatoan, who hath
journeyed with us from England, speaks our tongue and

doth act as peacemaker. There was blood spilt by our countrymen aforetime,

xxxxxxxxxxxxxxxxxxxxxxxxxxxxxxxxxxxxxxxxxxxxxxxxxxxx
xxxxxxxxxxxxxxxxx xxxx

xxxxxxxxxxxxxxxxxxxxxxxxxxxxxxxxxxxxxxxxxxxxxxxxxxxxx
amend what hath been done and seek friendship with those who know this land.

The 18th Day of August, 1587
This day hath brought forth joy unmatched: I, Eleanor Dare, daughter of the Governour and wife to Master Ananias Dare, was delivered of a daughter, here upon the soil of Virginia. The child was christened upon the Sunday following, and given the name Virginia, for she is the first Christian child borne unto English parents in this new land. I thank God for her safe coming.

The 22th Day of August, 1587
Today the whole of our company—xxxxxxxxxxxxxxxxxx and the planters—did gather before my Father and did entreat him earnestly to return to England, there to procure succour for us.

xxxxxxxxxxxxxxxxxxxxxxxxxxxxxxxxxxxxxxxx came too late in the season to plant any crop. Without aid, many fear xxxxxxxxxxxxxxxx the spring.

My Father's heart was heavy. He loves his granddaughter, little Virginia, and he did not wish to part xxxxxxxxxxxxxxxxxxxxxxxxxxxxxxxx

167

xxxxxxxxxxxxxxxxxxxxxxxxxxxxxxxxxxxxxxxxxx
xxxxxxxxxxxxxxxxxxxxxxxxxxxxxxxxxxxxx turn away from his
duty.

He made plan that we should remove our settlement
fifty miles into the maine, to a more secure
xxxxxxxxxxxxxxxxxxxxxxxxxxxxxxxxx from weather and
theft. There we are to dwell until his return.

Though my heart is sore at his
xxxxxxxxxxxxxxxxxxxxxxxxxxxxxxxxx he shall return
swiftly, and with all the aid we so dearly need.

The 27th Day of August, 1587
This day, my Father and nine others took sail back unto
England. Before his departure, we did agree upon a pact:
should we need to leave our dwelling, we would carve
into a tree the name of the place whither we had gone, so
that he might find us upon his return. If we must depart
hastily, a cross would be carved beside the name as a dire
warning.

The 8th Day of September, 1587
Throughout this autumn, we have moved our fort unto
the Cittie of Raleigh, as was decided with my Father. The
Croatoan have been most helpful and kind. They have
come unto us bearing food, and have welcomed
xxxxxxxxxxxxxxxxxxxxxxxxxxxxxxxxxxxxxxxxxxxxxxxxxxxx
xxxxxxxxxxxxxxxxxxxxxxxxxxxxxxxxxxxxxxxxxxxxxxxxxxxx

xxxxxxxxxxxxxxxxxxxxxxxxxxxxxxxxxxxxxxx and taught us to work the soil.

They are greatly taken with little Virginia, the first white child born upon this soil. They teach her their tongue, and we teach her English in return. Her blue eyes do marvel them, for such a colour they have never before beheld. xxxxxxxxxxxxxxxxxxxxxx my Father shall return with supplies, and our hearts are full of hope that we shall survive the coming winter.

The 25th Day of September, 1587
Manteo did remind xxxxxxxxxxxxxxxxx dreadful tale of the former settlers. Several years ago, another company of English did attempt to settle here. A silver cup was stolen by an Indian, and in anger, the English captured the chief of the Secotan, named Wingina, and did burn him alive before his village. They then set fire to the crops when the cup was not returned.

This cruel act set the Secotan against us, and Manteo was quick to warn me of this. Knowing my station as the xxxxxxxxxxxxxxxxxxxxxxxxxxxxxxxxxxxx the Secotan always with respect and kindness, hoping thereby to lead the others to do the same.

The 15th Day of October, 1587
On many occasions when we went to harvest our crops, we found them burning. The Secotan do make it their purpose xxxxxxxxxxxxxxxxxxxxxxxxxxxxxxxxxxxxxxxxxxxxxxxxxxx

xxxxxxxxxxxxxxxxxxxxxxxxxxxxxxxxxxxx out. Yet, whenever they sought to destroy us, the Croatoan stood beside us to aid and defend. Without their help, we surely would have perished.

Winter, 1588
Winter hath come harsh and cruel. The snows fell heavy, and the food hath been scarce.
xxxxxxxxxxxxxxxxxxxxxxxxxxxxxxxxx not for the generosity of the Croatoan, who saved us many times over.

We have lost five children to the fever, and four women are with child, two of whom are in great peril this cruel season. I fear they may not see the spring.

A strange beast hath wandered near the Citie. It is larger than a horse, with four legs, a great head covered in white woolly hair, and two horns upon its brow. The colonists believed it a gift from God to aid us in winter's grasp.

Manteo xxxxxxxxxxxxxxxxxxxxxxxxxxxxxxxxxxxx xxxxxxxxxxxxxxxxxxxxxxxxxxxxxxxxxxx xxxxxxxxxxxxxxxxxx xxxxxxxxxxxx xxxxxxxxxxxxxxxxxxxxxxxxxxxxxxxxxxx and its people.

The colonists did mock this warning and slew the buffalo to feed themselves. Yet, no fire would light, no xxxxxxxxxxxxxxxxxxxxxxxxxxxxxxxxxxxxxxxxxxxxxxxxx. The salt they had for curing meat vanished. Those who ate of the buffalo grew sick xxxxxxxxxxxxxxxxxxxxxxxx the Croatoan's healing, but help was denied.

Within three days, nearly half the colonists, forty-four souls, were dead, leaving only fifty-nine alive. A week hence, the buffalo disappeared. When morning came, it was gone without trace.

Spring, 1588
At last, spring hath xxxxxxxxxxxxxxxxxxxxxxxxx life. A child was born to Sara Payne and a Croatoan man named Tacumwah, wed this past summer. They named their son Orotam. Virginia and Orotam, close in age, xxxxxxxxxxxxxxxxxxxxxxxxxxxxxxxxxxxxxx.

My Father hath not returned as soon as we hoped. Though the winter was hard, we survived with the help xxxxxxxxxxxxxxxxxxxxxxxxxxxxxxxxxxxxxxxxxxxxxxxxxx xxxxx xxxxxxxxxxxxxxxxxxxxxxxxxxxxxxxxxxxxxxxxxxxxxxxx loss of forty-nine souls, from sickness and hunger. We began with one hundred fifteen men, women, and children; now but sixty remain, counting Virginia and Orotam.

Summer, 1588
We have been blessed with two more xxxxxxxxxxxxxxxxxxxxxxxxxxxxxxxxxxxxxxxxx parentage. We now have four Croatoan children with the rare blue-grey eyes living among us.

My Father's return remains uncertain. Many fear he hath perished upon the sea. Yet we cling to hope he will come back with supplies and new settlers.

Meanwhile,

xxxxxxxxxxxxxxxxxxxxxxxxxxxxxxxxxxxxxxxxxxxxxxxxxxx
xxxxxxxxxxxxxxxxxxxxxxxxxxx xxxxxxxxxxxxxxxxxxxxxxxxxx
xxxxxxxxxxxxxxxxxxxxxxxxxxxxxxxxxxxxxxxxxxxxxxxx.

The 18th Day of September, 1588
Knowing the coming winter shall be harsh once more, we
resolved to leave the Citie of Raleigh and dwell with
xxxxxxxxxxxxxxxxxxxxxxxxxxxxxxxxxxxxxxxxxxxxxxxxxx
xxxxx xxxxxxxxxxxxxxxxxxxxxxxxxxxxxxx CROATOAN"
upon a nearby palisade — the signal my Father and we
had agreed upon before his departure.

The 23th Day of September, 1588
Today we xxxxxxxxxxxxxxxxxxxxxxxxxxxxxxxx
xxxxxxxxxxxxxxxxxxxxxxxxxx xxxxxxxxxxxxxxxxxxxxxxxxx
xxxxxxxxxxxxxxxxxxxxxxxxxxxxxxxxxxxxxxxxxxxx the
Croatoan camp.

But fifteen miles from Raleigh, we were set upon by a
rival Indian faction, the Secotan. They came suddenly,
with bows and hatchets. Each of us seized our children
and fled through the woods, leaving all behind, fleeing
the screams and fury of the attack…

Nearly three hours had passed before Jenny finally set the
first journal down. She hadn't realized how deeply she'd been
drawn in—until the growing darkness reminded her the day had
slipped away. The fire had burned low, casting long shadows

across the living room. With a start, she stood to head outside and feed the horses.

As she reached for the back door, she found Tristan already stepping inside, shaking off the chill.

"I figured you were too wrapped up in that book to tear yourself away," he said with a grin. "Everyone's been fed and tucked in for the night."

Before she could respond, he leaned in and pressed a quick kiss to her cheek. "Go back to your mystery. I'll pick us up something for dinner."

And just like that, he was gone—out the front door before she could say a word. Jenny stood frozen for a beat, stunned by the unexpected gesture. It had been casual, friendly, maybe even sweet—but completely out of the blue.

She blinked, then turned back to the living room, unsure whether to be flustered or flattered. Before sitting down again, she grabbed a warm throw from the cedar chest and wrapped it around her shoulders.

Settling back onto the couch, she reached for the second journal. The cover was nearly identical to the first, though the stitching was looser and the leather slightly darker. As she opened it, she saw a familiar title page—almost the same words, but written in a different, firmer hand. It read:

Journal of Virginia Dare
1603

August 18, 1603

This day marks my sixteenth year, and my dear mother hath bestowed upon me this book, beseeching that I might record the chronicles of my life. I am Virginia Dare, daughter of Eleanor and Ananias Dare, and the first white child born in this New World.

I shall begin from the very start. As I have said, I was born in this strange and untamed land. When I was but three months old, my mother, father, and the others were journeying from xxxxxxxxxxxxxxxxxxxxxxxxxx xxxxxxxxxxxxxxxxxxxxxxxxxxxxxxxxxx xxxxxxxxxxxxxxxxxxxxxxxxxxxxxxxxxxxxxxx lands.

Many perished in that grievous attack, including my father. Oft I have wished to have known him, yet such wishes are but frivolous thoughts. My mother, Eleanor, hath raised me with care and courage. We now xxxxxxxxxxxxxxxxxxxxxxxxxxxxxxxxxxxxxxxxxx xxxxxxxxxxxxxxxxxxxxxxxx xxxxxxxxxxxxxxxxxxxx xxxxxxxxxxxxxxxxxxxxxxx.

April 13, 1604

My dear mother hath fallen grievously ill. She took a fever these past weeks. Small red spots doth appear upon her skin, and no quantity of fresh water or medicine hath brought her relief.

xxxxxxxxxxxxxxxxxxxxxxxxxxxxxxxxxxxx ill, many having passed from this world.

I remember well the council fashioning coffins for the little ones. They felled a great cypress tree and hollowed it as one would xxxxxxxxxxxxx. xxxxxxxxxxxxxxxxxxxxxxxxxxxx, then covered with another hollowed piece, thus enclosing the body. Deep in the earth these coffins were buried. The day was one of great sorrow.

April 21, 1604
My mother hath passed unto the Lord this day. Being Christians, the Croatoan made for her a xxxxxxxxxxxxxxxxxxxxxxxxxxxxxxxxxxxxxxxxxxxxx and the letters "I N R I," signifying "Jesus Nazarenus, Rex Judaeorum." Before sealing the coffin, I placed within her diary, that her words might rest with her.

xxxxxxxxxxxxxxxxxxxxxxxxxxxxxxxxxxxxxxxxxxxxx xx settlers living among the Croatoan, no more than fifteen souls. Many marriages have taken place between the white folk and the Croatoan, producing children fair of skin and grey of eye. Now that my mother is gone, I find myself all alone.

June 9, 1604
This day I shall wed my friend Caratoke. My heart rejoiceth, for at last I shall have a family of my own.

September 25, 1605
This blessed day, I xxxxxxxxxxxxxxxxxxxxxx, a boy and a

girl. Both have eyes of blue, like unto mine own, and skin lighter than my husband's. We have named them Pocosin and Wysocking, meaning Land xxxxxxxxxxxxxxxxxx xxxxxxxxxxxx tongue.

Winter, Anno Domini 1610

An elder of the Croatoan hath come to me bearing tidings of events past. There be two factions among xxxxxxxxxxxxxxxxxxxxxxxxxxxxxxxxxxxxxxxxxx Secotan. Before my mother and father came across the great ocean, xxxxxxxxxxxxxxxxxxxxxxxxxxxxxxxxxxx no peace with the Secotan. A stolen silver chalice brought discord; the Secotan were accused, and their leader was taken and cruelly burnt alive.

Thus the Secotan opposed further settlement, and did all in their power to drive us away. The xxxxxxxxxxxxxxxxxxxxxxx for a sign from their God. The elder told of a white buffalo that appeared upon the land, a wondrous sight sent to save us starving settlers.

The xxxxxxxxxxxxxxxxxxxxxxxxxxxxxxxxxxxxxxx warned against harming it. Yet the settlers, driven by xxxxxxxxxxxxxxxxxxxxxxxxxxxxxxx buffalo. This act incensed the Secotan, who cast a curse upon the beast and upon those who consumed it, bringing sickness and death.

To prevent further harm, the Croatoan secretly took the buffalo and buried it in a hidden place. The xxxxxxxxxxxxxxxxxxxxxxxxxxxxxxxxxxxxxxx a sacred union

176

between white and dark skins could heal the land and bring prosperity once more.

He declared that my children were this union, though I understand not fully the ways of the Croatoan. Yet I deem this tale worthy of record.

Summer, Anno Domini 1611

My children grow swiftly and show great strength and kindness. An elder returned to tell me of the gift they share. 'Tis he who xxxxxxxxxxxxxxxxxxxxxxxxxxxxx and the healing union.

He tells me Pocosin hath a xxxxxxxxxxxxxxxxxx beasts. If an animal be hurt, it seeketh her, and she healeth it. I find it difficult to believe, yet the elder is steadfast in his faith.

Wysocking, he says, guideth those xxxxxxxxxxxxx xxxxxxxxxxxxxxx in this world, helping them journey onward. Though such things seem magical to me, I cannot deny their wonder.

Autumn, Anno Domini 1611

If I had not witnessed it with mine own eyes, I would not have believed it. While walking with Pocosin among our horses, we spied a fox creeping through the tall grass. The fox gave xxxxxxxxxxxxxx by a startled horse and fell lifeless.

Pocosin approached the fallen creature and sang softly the songs taught her by the xxxxxxxxxxxxx great astonishment, the fox revived and walked away, whole once more. Truly, this is a miracle.

Winter, Anno Domini 1613
The winter grows harsh, and my strength wanes. I have taken ill with the same grievous fever that so xxxxxxxxxxxxxxxxxxxxxxxxxxxx spots have appeared upon my skin, and my body is weak beyond measure. By the counsel of the Elders and for the safety of all, I am set apart in a humble tent, distant xxxxxxxxxxxxxx xxxxxxxxxxxxxxxx aches sore for my dear children, Pocosin and Wysocking, whose laughter and presence have been the light of my days. I pray fervently to God that He will restore my health, that I might see them grow into the fullness of their gifts and purpose.

An hour later, the rich scent of garlic, soy, and sesame oil floated through the house—Jenny looked up, dazed from the pages of the journal. The aroma pulled her back to reality just as Tristan stepped through the door, arms full of Chinese takeout containers.

"You went all the way into town?" she asked, stunned.

Tristan grinned. "Only the best for a woman buried in history."

"Oh my God, Tristan!" she practically shouted, leaping off the couch, the journal still clutched in her hands. "You have *no* idea what I found!"

She dashed into the kitchen like a kid who'd just unwrapped the perfect gift on Christmas morning. Her excitement was contagious—her cheeks were flushed, her eyes wide with wonder.

"These journals," she said, waving one in front of him, "they belong to Eleanor and Virginia Dare!"

Tristan froze in place, the bags of food halfway onto the counter. "Wait. You mean *the* Eleanor and Virginia Dare? *Roanoke* Eleanor and Virginia Dare? As in '*The Lost Colony of Roanoke*' that we all learned in school about? THAT Eleanor and Virginia Dare?" He even did the air quotes.

Jenny nodded slowly, her gaze locked on his, her voice barely a whisper now. "I think we've found them, Tristan. Those coffins in the pasture—they might *belong* to them. I'm serious. We could be holding the key to solving one of America's oldest unsolved mysteries."

Tristan looked like he'd been hit with a bolt of lightning. "That's… incredible," he said, breathless.

Finally noticing the food, Jenny helped unpack the containers—hot and fragrant Chow Mein, Kung Pao chicken, and spring rolls. The smell stirred her appetite at last, and between eager bites, she began recounting what she'd read.

Tristan reached for one of the journals, and she slapped his hand away playfully. "No sauce on the 400-year-old relics, please."

Laughing, he leaned back. "So, the colonists didn't all vanish—they integrated with local tribes?"

"That's what the journals suggest," Jenny said, sipping her tea. "It makes sense. It could explain why so many Native Americans in this area have gray eyes."

"Like yours," Tristan said, almost offhandedly, continuing to eat his fried rice.

Jenny gave a small laugh, brushing it off. "I grew up in Boston, remember? I'm not exactly native to Virginia. But Jim Snyder, at the hardware store? And Dannie, over at the diner? They both have gray eyes. I wonder…"

"They could be descendants," Tristan said, nodding. "You should ask them sometime."

"Maybe I will," Jenny mused, looking thoughtful.

As they cleared the table together, Tristan asked, "So, what now? What are you going to do with the journals?"

Jenny placed the last plate in the dishwasher and closed it with a soft click. "I'm not sure. There's probably a historical society or museum that would kill to have them. But I don't want to exploit this—not for fame, not for money."

Tristan arched an eyebrow. "You sure you're not calling Geraldo Rivera?"

She gave him a playful shove. "Absolutely not."

"Good," he said, stepping closer. "Whatever you choose to do, I know it'll be the right thing."

She turned to face him fully, caught off guard by the seriousness in his eyes. Before she could respond, Tristan leaned in and kissed her—not a quick peck, but a slow, meaningful kiss that left her breathless.

When he pulled back, he smiled and said softly, "That one was on purpose."

Jenny blinked, stunned—and smiling.

~ ~ * ~ ~

The next evening, golden light filtered through the barn's high windows, casting long, dappled shadows across the straw-covered floor. Tristan moved with practiced ease among the stalls, scooping grain and portioning out hay, the rustle of feed bags and the soft snorts of the horses the only sounds breaking the silence.

Jenny leaned against the doorway, her arms folded, watching him work. Her mind was still turning over the events of the past few days—the unearthed coffins, the fragile, timeworn diaries, the ghosts of stories buried deep in both soil and memory.

As he secured the latch on the last stall, Tristan straightened, brushing his hands off on his jeans. "You know," he said casually, "my grandpa might still have some ties to the historical society down in Alabama. He used to do a lot with them—preservation projects, research, and old cemeteries. That kind of thing."

Jenny tilted her head, curiosity flickering in her eyes. "Really?"

"Yeah," Tristan nodded slowly. "I was thinking I could reach out to him—see if he knows anyone, maybe in Virginia, who could help us properly reinter the coffins. And also find a historical society that would be able to take care of the journals. Someone who understands how to handle all this... unusual stuff."

Jenny pushed off the doorframe, her pulse quickening. "That would be amazing, Tristan. This whole thing—it's bigger than us. We need help. The right kind."

"I'll talk to him tonight," he said, glancing out toward the fading horizon. "If anyone can stir up some answers from the past, it's him. He's like a walking archive, and he owes me a favor."

Jenny smiled, but the tension in her shoulders didn't ease. "Let's hope someone's still listening on the other end."

~ 18 ~

September 25th, 2029

Dew on the grass had turned to frost as Old Man Winter made an early entrance. By late September, a sudden cold front swept in from the north, dropping temperatures sharply. The weatherman hadn't predicted it, but moisture from the Atlantic collided with the cold, and by morning a light dusting of snow had begun to fall. Jenny woke to the sight of delicate white flakes drifting lazily to the ground.

Outside the patio door, she noticed small paw prints circling the backyard. Snookie had already explored the snowy grass, her trail weaving around the house and back into her doghouse, where she'd tucked herself away from the cold.

Jenny bundled up and headed out to feed the horses. She paused when she reached Galaxy's stall, taking a long look at the once-starved horse. In just three months, he had transformed. His ribs were no longer as visible, the hollows above his eyes had filled in, and his hips were rounding out. His coat shone with life, and the emptiness that had haunted his eyes was gone. He was alert, attentive—alive.

His left rear hoof was still healing, but the infection had cleared. Jenny had learned it could take up to a year for a hoof to fully regrow. Still, Galaxy had begun to play again. Most mornings, she let Yin and Yang into the pasture first, then opened the stall for Galaxy. Yang would take off in a full gallop, and Galaxy, with his longer strides, would soon catch up. He'd feint a nip at Yang's rear, prompting a playful buck in return. They'd chase each other, wild and free, until Yang returned to Yin, who waited calmly in the center. Despite her youth, Yin carried herself like the herd's matriarch.

That morning, Jenny lingered to watch their antics. The twins were enchanted by the snow, pawing and sniffing at it, sneezing when flakes tickled their noses. She laughed softly, content in this peaceful moment.

Happy and Zaar Aza emerged, unconcerned by the new scenery, but Johnnie refused to leave the warmth of the barn, peeking out and retreating back inside.

Tristan wasn't due for a few hours, and with Kirsten on vacation, Linda wouldn't be coming either. Jenny had the morning to herself. She left the barn's large door open so the horses could retreat inside if the snow became too much. After doing the morning chores, she curled up on the couch under her favorite blanket. The fireplace was on, but a chill still clung to the air. Misha, as always, found her place on Jenny's chest. Her rhythmic purring was a lullaby, and Jenny soon drifted off to sleep.

She woke to the screech of tires, a loud crunch of metal, and the piercing scream of a horse. Misha's claws dug into her chest as she bolted upright. Dazed, Jenny grabbed her phone and rushed outside. The sun had set, and a few more inches of snow blanketed the ground. The orange glow from streetlights bathed the landscape in a surreal light.

The sound of a blaring horn drew her across the pasture. What she found made her heart seize.

A large black Dodge pickup had skidded off the icy road, torn through her fence, and rolled into the field. A mangled 2-horse trailer was still attached. The truck had slammed into one of the horses and pinned it down. Galaxy.

Her heart screamed to rush to him, but her mind urged her to check the driver first.

"Sir, are you okay?" she called, standing at the crumpled door.

His face was bloodied, but his eyes were alert. "I'm alright, thanks to the airbag. Trapped, but nothing feels broken."

"I'll call for help," Jenny said quickly, then hesitated. "Are there any horses in the trailer?"

"No. It's empty. Probably why I slid—too light."

Relief flooded her, visible in the puff of her breath. She called 911, then rushed to Galaxy.

His hindquarters were pinned beneath the truck. Blood soaked the snow around him. He was thrashing, whinnying in agony. Jenny fell to her knees by his head, cooing softly, stroking his neck. She mimicked Paul's calming melody, hoping to bring him comfort. Her voice cut through his pain. He stopped struggling, eyes locked on her.

She called Paul. "Paul, please come quick. There's been an accident. Galaxy—" Her voice broke.

"Jenny, breathe," Paul said, calm but urgent. "What's happening?"

"A truck hit him. He's pinned. I've called 911, but I need help." She wiped tears from her cheeks.

"I'm on my way."

The sirens grew louder. She knew they weren't for Galaxy but for the driver. Still, she couldn't help the stab of selfish sorrow. Her horse—her beautiful, healing horse—was bleeding out in the snow.

Misha appeared, winding around Jenny, assessing the scene. She padded over to Galaxy and chirped. His body tensed, but her meowing seemed to soothe him. She licked his muzzle, curled against his cheek, their usual spot under the sun—and purred softly. Slowly, Galaxy stilled. His breathing slowed. His eyes fluttered closed.

Then the world began to shift.

The colors faded.

The brilliant white snow turned dull gray. The rich red of the blood went black in the frost. The flashing lights from the emergency vehicles bled together in spiraling slates of color— no longer red, white, and blue, but pale shadows of each. The air itself seemed to mute. All that remained was the rhythmic rise and fall of Misha's purring... and then, not even that. Galaxy was still.

He was gone.

"Ma'am. Ma'am!" A hand on her shoulder snapped Jenny out of the daze. She jerked her head up to see a firefighter crouched beside her. "Are you alright? Are you hurt?"

The touch grounded her. The colors came rushing back.

Red and blue lights flashed violently in her eyes. The snow was once again stark white. The blood—still there, vivid and dark—seared into her vision. She swallowed hard and shook her head. "No. I'm not hurt."

"We need to reach the driver. We'll move you somewhere safe." He placed a wool blanket around her and gently helped her to her feet.

Tristan came back to help with the evening chores, saw all the rescue apparatuses and went running across the pasture. "I saw the lights—what happened?"

Jenny's voice was barely audible. "Galaxy... he's... gone."

Tristan's face fell and surveyed the scene. He then took Jenny by the hand and led her to the tack room, sat her in the chair, then turned to care for the other horses. He gave each one an extra flake of hay.

Soon after, Paul's truck crunched down the icy drive. He entered the barn, just as Misha came running into the barn. Paul picked Misha up and closed her in his coat. He and Tristan spoke briefly, then Jenny followed them silently into the house.

She sat on the couch as Paul placed Misha on her lap. Tristan returned with a clean towel and sweatpants—Jenny's jeans were soaked in Galaxy's blood. She changed quietly.

Paul cleaned Misha's paws with care, checking for frostbite, drying her fur. Jenny came back and lay down, Misha curled into her lap, Tristan draped a blanket over them both.

Paul moved into the kitchen, making phone calls. Tristan disappeared again, returning minutes later.

"I cleaned Snookie's house. The blankets were soaked. I put down trash bags, towels, and some blankets so she can burrow. She's warm now."

Jenny hadn't even thought of Snookie.

Tristan flipped on the fireplace. The room warmed, and for the first time that night, Jenny let herself feel the full weight of grief.

~ ~ * ~ ~

Jenny had slept straight through the night, and when the scent of coffee reached her nose the next morning, it took her a moment to remember where she was. Disoriented, she rose from the couch and wandered into the kitchen. Something felt off. A heaviness hung in the air, and a knot tightened in her chest.

Then it hit her.

Galaxy was gone.

The memory struck like a blow, and her heart crumpled under the weight of it. Tears welled instantly. *Be strong… be strong…*

Ignoring the steaming mug of coffee waiting for her, she pulled on her coat and stepped outside. The cold air slapped her cheeks, waking her further, but not enough to shake the fog in her mind. She didn't register the horses calling from the barn. She didn't even notice Tristan's truck parked beside the house.

She only wanted one thing.

To see Galaxy.

Alive.

She forced herself across the frozen pasture toward the place where he had fallen. But the moment his lifeless form came into view, her emotions betrayed her and she once again began to cry.

The grief was unbearable. She knew Galaxy needed to be laid to rest, but she didn't know how to begin. Trembling, she called Paul. When he answered, all she could do was sob.

"Jenny, slow down," Paul said gently, his voice steady "I know it's hard, but I can't understand you." He waited for a few moments. "It's okay. I'm on my way. I'll be there soon."

She hadn't even considered that Paul might be grieving too.

Less than thirty minutes later, Paul arrived—followed shortly by a quiet caravan of trucks and cars that rolled gently up the drive.

He must have made some calls before coming.

Kimber, his vet tech, stepped out first. Behind her came a few volunteers from Beechland Animal Control, arms full of comfort. They brought warm muffins from Dannie's café, a few casseroles, and several pans of "heat and eat" meals—the universal language of loss.

Inside, they surrounded Jenny with quiet support. No one rushed her. They sat beside her, listened, held her when she cried. They grieved with her.

Outside, while Jenny was being cared for, others tended to Galaxy. Someone had brought a backhoe. With care and reverence, they laid him to rest in a grove of trees at the back of the property.

To the others, it seemed the most logical place.

But Jenny knew better.

It was the perfect place.

~ ~ * ~ ~

Jenny was drained long before evening came. The procession of people offering comfort, the smell of casseroles and coffee, the ache that hovered in every room—it all became too much. By 4 p.m., she climbed into bed and let the quiet darkness swallow her.

She woke up early the next morning to stillness. The kind that felt hollow.

She pulled on her coat and stepped into the cold. The instant chill kissed her cheeks and pressed against her skin, but it wasn't enough to numb the pain. That familiar, sickening void returned.

Galaxy was gone.

The grief struck fast and sharp, settling deep in her bones.

Jenny wandered toward the pasture. She stopped at the fence and climbed onto the middle plank, sitting on the top rung with her arms hugging her knees. Her eyes scanned the field. The newly repaired section of the fence was visible from where she sat, the wood still raw and pale. The ground was scarred— mud and snow churned by rescue vehicles and desperate footsteps.

And there, in the distance, a faint rust-colored stain marked the earth.

Jenny's breath caught. She couldn't go closer. Her body wouldn't let her.

Then came footsteps. Slow, deliberate. The soft crunch of boots on frost. She didn't turn. She didn't need to.

Tristan's arms wrapped around her from behind. His warmth blanketed her back, his breath brushing her cheek. She leaned into him, her head falling against his chest.

"I'm so sorry," he whispered, voice rough with sorrow. "About Galaxy."

Jenny turned and melted into his arms. His embrace was strong and steady. She gripped his jacket tightly, anchoring herself. His scent—earthy, clean, familiar—wrapped around her, grounding her in something real. Her tears came without asking. Not loud. Just steady. Quiet. Painful.

Tristan held her tighter. She felt him trembling, too. This grief wasn't hers alone.

She wasn't alone.

When her sobs began to fade and the ache shifted into something less sharp, he touched her chin and lifted her face. His green eyes searched hers with a tenderness that broke her heart all over again.

He leaned in slowly. She met him halfway.

Their lips brushed once, tentative, then again, deeper. She curled her fingers into his coat, clinging to him, and kissed him harder. It wasn't just comfort—it was need. Desperate, aching need.

Tristan's hands slid to her waist. He lifted her from the fence in one smooth motion, and she wrapped her legs around his hips without hesitation. He carried her across the pasture to the back of the barn, shouldering open the door.

Inside, he grabbed the wool blanket from the day before and headed up the loft stairs. The hay-sweet air wrapped around them, and in the dim, golden light, they became something fragile and whole.

Tristan laid out the blanket over a bed of hay and sat down, pulling her into his lap. They kissed again—slower now, but no less urgent. Her hands tangled in his hair. His breath hitched as she pressed against him, her thighs tightening around his waist. He slid her coat from her shoulders, his fingers trembling as he found the buttons of her shirt. She pulled his sweater over his head, trailing kisses down the curve of his neck.

Their clothes fell away, piece by piece. Skin met skin in the soft hush of morning. The world narrowed to the warmth of his hands, the heat in her chest, the steady rhythm of their breathing as he laid her back on the blanket.

He entered her slowly, reverently, his lips still on hers, his hands holding her like something precious. Jenny gasped, not from pain, but from release—release of grief, of fear, of everything she'd been holding in.

They moved together, a quiet dance of mourning and comfort, of two souls trying to remember how to feel alive again. The hay rustled beneath them. Frost glistened on the loft window. Outside, the snow was starting to melt.

Jenny clung to him, tears mixing with breathless gasps, and in that moment, wrapped in Tristan's arms, she felt something she hadn't since before the accident—safe.

~ ~ * ~ ~

Three days after the accident, Jenny finally returned to her usual routines—though nothing about life on the farm felt *usual* anymore. The rhythm had changed, a subtle but undeniable shift in the air. Grief had settled over the land like a heavy fog, muting everything it touched. Even the animals felt it.

Each morning, the barn greeted her with a silence that was louder than any sound. The horses, once lively and playful, now stood quietly in their stalls, their heads low, their eyes dulled. They no longer raced through the pasture or teased one another at feeding time. Their appetites had diminished, and the joyful energy that once defined their days was gone, replaced by a shared, quiet mourning.

But no one grieved more visibly than Misha.

Jenny found her curled in Galaxy's empty stall each night, a small, unmoving shadow in the shavings. She no longer came running when Jenny entered the barn, didn't meow or nuzzle or ask to be held. She refused food, even when Jenny brought it to her directly. Her once-glossy coat had started to fall out in patches, and she shrank away from touch when Jenny tried to clean her.

It broke Jenny's heart all over again.

Worried, she finally called Paul. But after a long pause, his voice was gentle.

"There's nothing I can really do for her," he said. "She's grieving, Jenny. Just like the rest of us. And sometimes... animals need space to mourn, too."

Jenny knew he was right, but it didn't make it any easier to watch.

Everything on the farm still moved—time, chores, the changing sky—but it all moved slower now. Dimmer. Quieter.

And Galaxy's absence echoed in every corner.

~ ~ * ~ ~

Three days later, with the grief still sharp and unrelenting, Mary called with news that hit Jenny like a fresh bruise.

Yin and Yang were ready for adoption.

Jenny had known the day would come, but it didn't make it any easier. They had helped keep her afloat in the days after Galaxy's death, their playful antics and innocent energy a balm to her broken heart. The thought of their empty stalls was almost unbearable—there was already one too many.

It took less than a day to find a family.

When they arrived, Jenny couldn't help but notice how picture-perfect they looked: a smiling mother and father, and twin girls—Cindy and Sandy—about eight years old, with matching freckles and eyes full of mischief. Jenny could tell, instantly, they were the type to swap places and cause playful chaos at school. The kind of girls who would grow up with endless stories of harmless tricks and summer adventures.

Jenny felt a sharp pang of envy. They had what she had always dreamed of: a whole family, intact. Parents who clearly adored them. A sister to share secrets and laughter with. Her childhood, by contrast, had felt like a puzzle with too many missing pieces. No siblings. No parents after she turned ten. Only Uncle Brian, well-meaning but distant, too absorbed in work to fill the spaces left behind.

And always, horses had been her secret wish.

As a girl, she had devoured every horse book she could find, taped posters to her walls, and circled listings in the *Little Nickel Want Ads* like they were windows into another life. Every Saturday, she'd walk six blocks to grab a copy of the yellow paper, sprawl in front of the TV with the volume on low, red marker in hand, and circle every "Free Horse" ad she could find. When her parents said they didn't have the space, she circled ads for land. When they said they couldn't leave Boston, she tried to find listings near the city. Always trying. Always hoping.

But the answer had always been no.

Even with Uncle Brian, the dream remained out of reach. There was never enough space, never enough time. So, she had grown into a woman with the heart of a horse-crazy girl, always carrying that quiet ache.

And now, watching Cindy and Sandy fall in love with Yin and Yang at first sight, Jenny could see herself in them. She recognized the wide-eyed wonder, the quiet reverence in how they reached out to touch soft noses and giggled when the yearlings nuzzled them back. Yin and Yang had outgrown their shared stall and were now housed side by side. Cindy immediately bonded with Yin, Sandy with Yang—no confusion, no debate. Just instinct. Jenny had to smile through the ache.

As the foals were led into the trailer, the sound of the doors latching shut echoed too loudly in Jenny's ears. Grief surged again, sudden and fresh. Galaxy. Now Yin and Yang. Her barn, once so full of life, grew quieter by the day.

She wrapped her arms around herself against the wind and the weight of it all.

These horses were never *just* rescues. They were her babies. The family she had chosen, or perhaps, the one that had chosen her. After her third miscarriage, a doctor had quietly, compassionately told her the truth—she would never carry a child to term. She had left that appointment hollowed out. For a long time, there had been only silence.

Then the animals started arriving.

And slowly, piece by piece, they filled that silence. They gave her a purpose, a way to love, to nurture, to heal. They gave her something to hold onto.

Now, she was letting more of them go.

But this time, as she waved to the family pulling out of the driveway, she felt something else, too—a sliver of comfort. Yin and Yang were going to two little girls who would love them like she once dreamed of loving a horse. And that, somehow, felt like a full-circle kind of grace.

Still, the ache remained.

But so did the love.

~ 19 ~
Grove of Ghosts

October 2029

Two weeks after the accident, the ache in Jenny's chest hadn't lessened, but her mind had begun whispering what her body refused to hear: *Get up. Move. Breathe.*

It was just after 3 p.m., the sun had already begun its slow descent. Shadows stretched long across the snow as Jenny pulled on her boots and jacket. The barn chores were covered—Tristan had taken care of everything that morning. She'd insisted he take the night off. He'd agreed too easily, and Jenny suspected it was his way of nudging her toward the rhythm of living again, a gentle reminder that she was still needed. Still capable.

She turned away from the barn and walked across the field toward the grove.

Galaxy's grave rested near its edge—no marker, only a soft rise in the snow-covered earth, like the land itself had exhaled around him. Though buried in the pasture, it felt like the grove had claimed him, stretching out its arms and folding him into its quiet protection.

Jenny didn't linger. Standing too long at his grave always tore open wounds that hadn't even begun to scar. Instead, she kept walking, vaulting over the fence and disappearing into the trees.

The grove hadn't changed. The air inside was still and heavy, as if the world outside didn't exist. The winter birds had gone quiet, and a hush fell like a blanket over everything.

Then she saw it — movement. A shadow gliding between the birches, smooth and dark against the bright snow. It wasn't menacing. If anything, it felt familiar. Comforting.

A breeze stirred, barely more than a breath, and carried a high, drifting sound with it — a note that brushed the edge of her memory. It teased her brain, the way a name sits just out of reach.

She followed the shadow deeper into the grove.

It led her, almost playfully, until the trees opened into the heart of the woods. A massive birch stood in the center, its white bark marred by two carvings. The first was clear: **C R O**. The second—a crude image that looked like a buffalo, or something close, like a child's idea of one carved with uncertain hands.

A wave of nausea hit her. She bent over and vomited into the snow, trembling, breath clouding in front of her.

What was this place? And why did it feel like it remembered her?

The light was fading fast. The forest had swallowed the sun. The stars blinked awake above the canopy, but with no clouds to hold in the warmth, the air dropped into a biting chill. She had no flashlight, no phone, and no one knew where she was.

She turned to leave—at least, she thought she did—but something felt wrong. The trees looked unfamiliar, every direction the same. A creeping sense of dread spread through her chest.

She was lost.

Just as panic began to rise, she saw the shadow again, about thirty yards ahead. It moved slowly now, gliding just at the edge of her vision. Another gust of wind passed over her, colder this time, laced again with that sound—a thin, downward-drifting note.

There it is… I know that sound…

But it slipped away again before she could name it.

She followed the shadow carefully, picking her steps to avoid twisting an ankle. Her breath fogged heavily in the air, her legs burning with cold. The trees began to thin, and the sky opened wider above her. She was leaving the grove. She could feel it.

Then, finally, she heard it again—clear, distinct: a whinny.

Galaxy's whinny.

She froze.

It was faint, too faint to be any of the horses still in the barn. Still, it filled her chest with a sudden warmth. She turned toward the sound and saw the pasture fence. The moonlight glowed off the snow, guiding her like a lantern.

She climbed the fence and crossed the pasture. No horses were out.

A flicker of anxiety surged—had they escaped?

She rushed to the barn and threw open the door.

They were all there.

Zaar Aza, Happy, Johnnie—all content, standing in their own stalls, eating their dinner. They'd been inside for nearly an hour. None of them even lifted their heads at her entrance, as if she hadn't been gone at all. Tristan must have come and done the evening feeding, without her even knowing.

Jenny exhaled, relief giving way to confusion.

Then whose whinny had I heard?

She moved to Galaxy's stall and found Misha curled in the corner, buried beneath wood shavings like a wounded ghost. Jenny knelt beside her. The cat stirred, slowly rising to press her paws against Jenny's chest. Her eyes—once dull and yellowed—held a glimmer of green again. A spark of the Misha she had known. She rubbed her cheek against Jenny's, licked her once, then turned and disappeared into the mound of shavings.

Jenny reached out, touched the soft fur between Misha's ears, and whispered something she didn't know she was going to say.

"I miss him too."

The food and water dishes were full, untouched. Misha's body had grown frail—her spine and hip bones too pronounced, her coat matted with neglect. She hadn't eaten since Galaxy's death.

The next morning, when Jenny returned to the barn, she knew before entering that something had changed.

Misha didn't stir when she opened the stall.

She was still curled up in the same spot, eyes closed. Peaceful. Still.

Misha had died of a broken heart.

Tears welled in Jenny's eyes, but she didn't cry right away. Instead, she knelt beside the cat who had never left Galaxy's side, even in death. She stroked the soft fur and whispered her goodbye.

Later that afternoon, Paul came by. Together, they buried Misha as close to Galaxy as they could, under the same sky, near the same trees.

"I hope they find each other," Jenny said quietly, brushing snow from her coat.

Paul nodded. "If anyone could… it'd be those two."

And beneath the soft hush of the grove, Jenny swore she heard it again—that faint, drifting sound.

A whinny, far away.

But not lost.

~ 20 ~
Dinner with Grandma

October, 2029

By mid-October, dew had given way to frost. Autumn had sharpened its edge, and the nights were bitter enough to rattle the windows. Jenny was curled under a blanket when her phone rang. It was Paul.

"Hey," he said. "My grandmother wants you to come by for tea today."

Jenny raised her eyebrows. "Why?"

"I talk to her every week, keep her updated on what's happening around here… and that now includes you. I told her about the accident, the horses… everything. She said she needs to see you. I'll pick you up at four?"

There was no hesitation. "Sure." Curiosity outweighed any discomfort.

The drive was quiet, almost reverent. Paul didn't offer small talk, and Jenny sensed he was holding something back—letting the moment arrive on its own, without interference.

When they pulled up to a small, weathered house tucked into a wooded bend in the road, Jenny felt a shift in the air. Smoke curled from the chimney, and the faint smell of cedar and bread floated out as Paul opened the door.

"Come in, child," came a voice from inside—low, rich, and cracked with age.

The home was modest, more cabin than house. Four plain walls surrounded by shelves filled with feathers, jars of dried herbs, and small hand-carved figures. A fire flickered in a stone hearth. The warmth wrapped around Jenny the moment she stepped inside.

The old woman stood waiting, a soft smile lifting her face as she extended a hand, rings of turquoise and bone glinting on her fingers. Her hair was long and white, braided loosely down her back. Her face was a map of deep lines and sun-darkened skin. Her eyes, however—pale gray and unblinking—were alive with sharp light, as if lit from within.

She led Jenny into a small living room. Jenny was guided gently to sit on a faded couch, while the elder lowered herself with surprising grace to the floor, cross-legged, her skirt pooling around her like a woven river.

Paul stayed quiet, leaning against the doorframe.

"My name is Niskadi," she said, voice like wind over dry leaves. "It means 'she who listens to the trees.' My grandmother's mother gave it to me when I was still inside my own mother. Names are not chosen lightly."

Jenny nodded, unsure whether she should speak.

Niskadi began to speak without ceremony, her words weaving slowly, as if from memory and dream.

"My great-great-great-grandmother passed down this story," she said, her voice low and steady, like the wind whispering through pine. "When the white man first came to our lands, they brought many things. Some were gifts. Most were wounds.

"They brought war—not only against us, but against themselves. Still, we welcomed them, our arms open like the river welcomes the sky.

"Even after the blood spilled, we opened our arms.

"They brought sickness—illnesses that swept through our villages like wildfire, taking our children, our grandmothers, our warriors. Still, we opened our arms.

"They took our lands, the very earth beneath our feet, the ground where our ancestors sleep. They took our sacred places, our homes, our way of living.

"And still…"—her eyes held Jenny's— "…we opened our arms.

"When the first of the white men came, the Shaman was given a vision. The eagle spirit came to him in the wind, circling high, then landing low beside the fire.

"The spirit said, 'Do not raise your weapons. Do not meet them with anger. There must be peace between your people and theirs. A union must be made—of blood, of spirit, of heart. Only then will Mother Earth find her balance again.'

"From this union, the spirit said, would come children touched by the sacred. One would carry the gift to heal the wounded—of flesh and soul. The other would guide the lost, walking between worlds to help them find their way.

"After the visions were given, a sacred sign followed. Into our village came the white buffalo — pure as snow, eyes deep with knowing. To our people, the white buffalo is a gift from the Creator, a promise of good fortune, of healing, of plenty.

"But the white man, hungry and lost in their own ways, did not see what we saw. They killed the sacred one, thinking only of their empty bellies.

"With its death, the blessings turned to burdens. Mother earth turned her face from us—our crops withered; the horses scattered like leaves in the wind. And those who ate the sacred meat grew sick, for what is holy cannot be taken without cost.

"To bring balance back to the land, my people moved under the cover of night. They took the sacred remains of the White Buffalo, carrying them quietly away from the eyes of those who did not understand. In a place hidden from the world, they laid the buffalo to rest once more, hoping to soothe the restless spirit they had disturbed.

"But the land remembers. The earth holds the memory, and it does not forget so easily.

"The Shaman said, 'These troubles came with the White People, yet they too are children of the Creator and must be protected.'

"The Secotan held deep distrust for the White People and saw this as reason enough to strike back. They were fierce and cunning hunters, and many of the White People fell before they reached my people, the Algonquin. But my ancestors showed mercy and saved those who survived the battle."

With that, Niskadi voice grew soft, and her story came to rest.

"Wow, Grandma. Quite the story!" Paul interjected.

"PJ! Shush! Not done..." she smiled but only looked directly at Jenny. "I understand you've found some journals?"

This piqued Jenny's interest. "Yes! I did! How did you..."

Niskadi eyes flitted towards Paul.

"I have something for you."

She stood, slowly, and disappeared into another room. Jenny looked at Paul, who shrugged his shoulders.

Niskadi returned holding a small wooden box, its surface dark and smooth with age, hand-carved with spirals and feather symbols. She placed it gently in Jenny's lap, saying, "This has been passed down from generation to generation, to me, to give to the right spirit that should come during my time."

"Thank you," Jenny said, surprised by the weight of the box—and of the moment. "But... are you sure? This looks important. It should stay with your family."

Niskadi pressed the box back into Jenny's hands firmly. "This *is* staying with family. Now, you are part of that line, too. Not by blood. By purpose."

Jenny looked to Paul, expecting protest. He only watched quietly, eyes on the box.

She opened the lid slowly.

Inside was a small, leather-bound notebook. Its edges gilded with fading gold leaf, nearly identical to the ones she had found in the riven coffins—only smaller. More personal.

Jenny turned the cover, careful not to damage the delicate pages. Her fingers trembled.

"This," Niskadi said softly, "has been waiting for the right hands. And they are yours."

Journal of John White
1590

Jenny looked up at Grandma, amazed at this find. She knew immediately that this journal was from the grandfather and father of the two journals she had in her possession. What a rare find! She couldn't wait to get home and read this one! But more than that, she couldn't wait to tell Tristan!

"I... I don't know what to say, except thank you!" Jenny reached out to hug Grandma. Jenny was so excited and thrilled. She couldn't wait to tell Tristan what she had received.

~ ~ * ~ ~

On the ride home, she side-eyed Paul, "So... "PJ" huh?" she quipped with a smirk.

"Yeah, Grandma always called me PJ, for Paul, Jr. Since Paul was my father." She's the ONLY one allowed to call me that, so don't get any ideas!" Paul quipped. "By the way, I ran into Mary at the diner the other day and she reminded me of the big Gala that's coming up next month. She wanted to make sure you knew about it, and that you were invited."

"Gala?" Jenny asked. "What's it for?"

"It's a big to-do around here. This year will be the 10th Annual Beechland's Best Friends Gala – A Night for the Animals! It's a huge fundraiser we do for the Animal Shelter, and Animal Control. And, since you're technically a foster, you should be there! It also celebrates all the hard work we all do for the animals."

"Wow! Sounds like a fun night!! Can I bring a date?" she asked. "Is it formal?" she quickly interjected to maybe take the weight off the previous question.

"Yes, you can bring a date. The dress is usually cowboy formal. Which means your best jeans, cowboy boots and cowboy hats."

~ 21 ~
Johnnie Be Good

November, 2029

"Jenny… I've got some good news and bad news. What do you want to hear first?" Mary asked over the phone one afternoon.

"How about the good!" Jenny answered.

"I'm not sure if you've heard, but we have a Gala every year, it's a fundraiser for the animals in our County. We hold it in the big barn behind Dannie's Diner every year. I really want you to come."

"I'd love to! And yeah, Paul told me about a little while ago. Can I bring anyone with me?" Jenny asked.

"Of course you can! But it better be that stud of a ranch-hand you have over there! You're hiding him away all to yourself, and inquiring minds want to know!" Mary quipped.

"Inquir- Minds – What exactly do they want to know?" Jenny asked.

"Well, if there is any hay making going on in the hay in your barn! Of course!" Mary said with a grin.

"Well, since I don't kiss and tell, they will just have to keep guessing! What's the bad news?" Jenny quickly asked, changing the subject.

"Yes, the bad news," Mary's voice cracked over the phone. "The judge gave custody of Johnnie Walker back to his original owner this morning. He convinced the court it was the trainer who abused him, claimed he had no idea what was happening."

Jenny froze.

"And the judge bought it," Mary continued, her voice thick with frustration. "He actually believed him. He said he's coming this afternoon to—" she paused, disgusted, "'collect his goods.' That's what he called Johnnie. I'm so sorry, Jenny."

The world tilted.

Jenny couldn't breathe. Words failed her, slipping through the chaos in her mind like water through fingers. Anger. Shock. Disbelief. None of it captured the storm inside her. A wave of nausea hit, and she stumbled to the bathroom, barely making it before her stomach revolted.

When it was over, she gripped the sink, shaking.

No.

She stared at her reflection—eyes wide, face pale, jaw clenched. That man wasn't taking Johnnie. Not without going through her first. Not without a fight. She called Tristan for back-up.

A few hours later, a gleaming silver extended cab truck rolled up the drive, a glossy 3-horse trailer hitched to the back like a threat. Jenny stood near the barn, her arms crossed, heart pounding, but thankful Tristan showed up to help. Someone needed to be the buffer—or the leash.

Tristan stepped forward as the truck came to a halt. The man who climbed out was older, heavyset, with white hair who looked like he hadn't seen a saddle in years. He chewed on a toothpick and ignored Tristan's offered hand.

"Where's MY BrandyWine?" the man asked flatly, eyes scanning the property with smug entitlement.

Tristan didn't flinch. "You mean Johnnie Walker? Interesting name you had for him. What does it mean?"

The man didn't reply, just raised an eyebrow like he was above small talk.

"Here's the thing," Tristan said, calm as ever. "I'd like to buy him from you. What's he worth?"

The old man chuckled, shifting the toothpick between his teeth. "Worth a lot. He's a money-maker, that one. Pulled in a five-grand purse once."

Tristan nodded, sizing him up. "Alright. How about six thousand? Cash. You leave him here, no hard feelings "

The man scratched his head, finally looking at Tristan, clearly was tempted. He saw dollar signs and held out his hand—palm up, not for a handshake, but for the money.

"I'll take it out of your bill," Tristan said casually.

"Bill?" The man's brow furrowed. "What bill?"

"Well, let's see." Tristan leaned against a fence post. "Three months of boarding, feed, medical care—your horse was in pretty rough shape when he got here."

"You never got my permission for any of that," the man snapped.

"No, you're right," Tristan said coolly. "We could've left him to suffer. But we didn't. So, now we're owed. Let's break it down, shall we?" He pulled his ball cap off, scratched his head as if doing math in the air. "Boarding and feed? $750 a month. Vet bills—those were steep. Close to $7,000. Then the rehab, easily another $3,000."

Jenny watched from the sidelines, her grin slowly spreading as she caught on to the game.

"So, $750 times three…plus the rest…" Tristan tilted his head thoughtfully. "Yeah, that puts us around twelve grand. Meaning, after your six-thousand offer, you still owe us another six."

He paused, then added, "You can make the check out to Jenny Ritter. That's Jenny with a 'J'."

The man's bravado deflated. He scratched the back of his neck, eyeing the trailer, then the barn.

"Well…" he finally muttered. "How about you just keep the damn hay burner, and we'll call it even?"

Tristan offered his hand again—this time sideways, a proper shake, but the man still refused.

"Deal," Tristan said, his tone steady.

He stepped into the feed room, came back with a pad of paper, and wrote out a quick Bill of Sale. The man signed it without another word.

By the time he drove off, empty trailer rattling behind him, Jenny could hear him grumbling all the way down the driveway.

Tristan folded the signed paper into his jacket pocket, then turned to Jenny with a shrug. "Guess I own a horse now."

Jenny exhaled, the first deep breath in hours, and smiled.

"I can't believe you actually did that!" Jenny laughed, rushing forward and throwing her arms around Tristan. She gave him a quick kiss on the lips, grateful, and full of hope.

He hugged her back briefly, then pulled away, his tone resolute. "There was no way I was letting Johnnie go back to that man. To him, the horse was just property. But Johnnie... he's too special for that. Even if he still won't let anyone get close."

Tristan pulled a folded slip of paper from his jacket and handed it to her.

"What's this?" Jenny asked, unfolding it. Her eyes widened. "Wait—you can't do that. This is a rescue, not a boarding facility. I'm just a foster home."

"Sure I can," Tristan said with a shrug. "He's mine now. And I want to give him to you."

"Tristan, I can't afford him," she said, shaking her head. "I own the land and the house, yeah—but I don't have a job. Beechland Animal Control covers feed and vet bills for the rescues. That's the deal. I just provide the space and care."

"You give more than that," he said softly. "You give these animals a second chance. You give them peace."

He looked around the barn, then back at her. "Okay, how about this? I keep him. But I board him here. You run the show; I pay the bills. What's a fair monthly rate?"

Jenny paused, making a quick mental tally. "Uh... maybe $250?"

"Done," Tristan said. "Let's call it $2,000 a month."

She blinked. "What?"

"Until I find him a good home," he added with a grin. "Which, let's be honest, might take a very long time."

Jenny opened her mouth to protest but stopped herself. Instead, she smiled—really smiled—and nodded. "Deal."

Just then, Linda emerged from the barn, gently leading Johnnie Walker on a long line. The horse followed her step for step, calm and steady. She strolled toward the tall grass behind the house—grass Jenny had never quite found time to mow. In one hand, Linda carried a worn paperback, her favorite pastime lately: reading aloud while Johnnie grazed.

"I think I just found that new home…" Tristan murmured, so softly it was almost lost to the breeze. With a smile spreading across his face, he walked toward Linda and sat beside her in the grass.

Jenny followed, staying just close enough to hear without interrupting.

"What are you reading?" Tristan asked.

"Black Beauty," Linda said proudly, holding up the book.

"Classic," he grinned. "One of my favorites, too. What do you think—does Johnnie Walker like it here?"

"Oh yeah," Linda nodded. "He doesn't have to bend down too far. The grass is tall and sweet. He's a tall boy."

Tristan chuckled. "You're right about that. Do you think you could take care of him… forever?"

Linda looked at him, puzzled for a moment. "I already do. I'm here every day."

He nodded. "I know. But what I mean is—what if he was yours? What if Johnnie Walker was your horse?"

Linda went still, eyes wide. She stared at Tristan, as if waiting to see if he was serious.

"I'd help with everything," he added gently. "Food, vet bills—whatever you need. He'd be yours, but you wouldn't be alone."

Linda's brow furrowed as she processed his words, then slowly, her face began to light up. The corners of her mouth twitched, rising higher and higher until her whole expression radiated pure joy. She understood. And she was overjoyed.

Jenny watched, her throat tightening with emotion. The right horse had found the right heart.

As fall came to a close, it was time for Kirsten to leave for her first year of college. With her departure, things were changing at the farm—most notably, Linda would no longer be helping with daily chores as Kirsten was her daily chauffer to the barn. Johnnie Walker would be leaving too. Fortunately, one of Linda's neighbors offered to board Johnnie at their place, just down the road, so Linda could walk down and visit him every day. Tristan had insisted on covering the costs, but the neighbors wouldn't hear of it. Linda had grown up next door; she wasn't just a neighbor to them—she was family.

The barn was growing quieter by the day. With each empty stall, Jenny found herself with more free time—time that wasn't a relief, but a reminder. Time that she spent grieving. Not only the losses to death, but the ones to new beginnings. Even though Yin, Yang, and Johnnie were off to good, loving homes, she still missed them deeply. Now, only Happy and Zaar Aza remained in the barn.

There was comfort, at least, in watching Happy and Zaar Aza bond. They were like two old souls who had found each other late in life, kindred spirits easing each other's burdens. Zaar Aza had taken to his role as Happy's seeing-eye companion with gentle grace, as though he'd known it was his purpose all along.

Jenny was standing at the fence, watching the horses graze when a question suddenly popped into her head. "Tristan, how many hours of Community Service do you have left?"

Tristan looked down and his muddy boots, a little embarrassment in his voice, "Honestly, they were done two months ago! I really like what you are doing here Jenny, " he said, and he pulled in next to her. "What you do here matters." He placed a hand gently on the small of her back—a simple gesture of support, but it lingered just long enough to suggest something more. Comfort, yes... but with the soft edge of something deeper, something intimate.

"Don't you have a movie to prep for, or a script to read? Anything *Hollywood* at all to do?" Jenny teased, glancing at him with a sideways smile.

Tristan leaned against the fence beside her, one boot crossed over the other, arms resting casually on the top rail. "Actually," he said, his voice quieter now, "I'm taking a break from acting."

218

That surprised her. She turned to look at him fully, eyebrows raised.

He didn't flinch under her gaze. "Trying to re-evaluate some things. Rethink what I want out of all this. The spotlight, the hustle, the whole circus." He gestured vaguely toward the open sky, as if Hollywood itself were hiding behind the clouds. "Watching you out here—actually making a difference with these lives, day in and day out—it's made me realize I want to do more of that. Something real. Something that feels like it matters. And it does. It feels good."

Jenny looked away, her eyes drifting to where Happy and Zaar Aza were grazing peacefully. Her heart gave a quiet twist. She wasn't used to people saying things like that to her — especially not people like *him*. Movie stars didn't usually care about muddy boots and feed schedules, let alone what it meant to save a life that couldn't thank you.

"You're not what I expected, you know," she said finally.

He smiled. "Yeah, I get that a lot."

Jenny let out a soft laugh, shaking her head. "I mean it. I figured you'd serve your community service, smile for the cameras, and disappear back to your L.A. mansion the second your hours were up."

"I do miss the heated floors," he said, grinning. "But this," he nodded toward the pasture. "This sticks with me more than I expected."

There was a long pause.

The wind shifted, warm and easy, carrying the scent of hay and wildflowers.

And in that stillness, Jenny felt something settle between them. Not heavy. Not urgent. Just *real*.

Jenny's fingers curled loosely around the fence rail, her voice quieter now. "Most people don't stick around when life gets messy. It's easier to care from a distance, or just plain leave."

Tristan tilted his head, watching her. "Not sure if you've notice, but I haven't left."

She glanced at him, a little wary, a little hopeful. "I think you're surprising me. And I don't get surprised much."

He took a small step closer. Not dramatic, just enough to close a bit of the space between them. "I don't want to be just a surprise. I want to be someone you trust."

Jenny's heart beat a little faster at that. Trust wasn't something she handed out easily — too many broken promises, too many people who'd meant well but left anyway. But Tristan… he kept showing up. With muck on his boots, hay in his hair, and that ridiculous movie-star smile that somehow didn't feel fake when he was standing here, fence-line deep in the middle of her world.

"You're not exactly subtle," she said, raising an eyebrow.

"Wasn't trying to be."

His gaze didn't waver. And then—almost like a question, almost like a promise—his hand brushed hers where it rested on the rail. The touch was light, tentative. Giving her room to pull away.

She didn't.

Instead, she turned her hand slightly, letting her fingers slip into his. The warmth of it was startling, like the sun breaking through on a cold day.

Tristan let out a quiet breath, like he hadn't realized he'd been holding it.

For a moment, they just stood there, watching the horses graze under the wide-open sky. Nothing needed to be said. Not yet.

But Jenny felt something shift—not like a sudden change, but a gate slowly opening. A space she hadn't let anyone into in a long time. And for the first time in what felt like forever, she didn't feel the need to close it.

~ ~ * ~ ~

Then came the morning that shattered the quiet rhythm of winter.

Jenny stepped into the barn for the usual breakfast feeding, but something felt wrong—off. The air was too still. The usual soft nickers of greeting from Happy and Zaar Aza were absent. Silence met her instead.

Flicking on the lights, she scanned the barn. Happy stood in his stall, motionless, head low. Her heart sank. She rushed forward and found Zaar Aza lying down, still and silent. She dropped to her knees beside him.

He was alive—barely. His eyes opened when she touched him, and in them, Jenny saw the unmistakable glimmer of pain. She reached for her phone, fumbling through her coat pocket.

221

Then, just as she found it, the colors around her began to shift. The warmth of the barn turned to muted grays. The golden shavings, the chestnut of Zaar Aza's coat, even the black of his mane—all faded into a soft, lifeless monochrome.

He took one final breath. Deep. Long. Then slowly let it go.

And then—nothing.

The color returned all at once. Jenny's vision cleared, but her chest felt hollow as she dialed Paul's number.

"Paul… I need… something. I don't know what," she said, the words breaking under the weight of her sobs.

"What is it, Jenny?" Paul asked, concern deepening his voice.

"I think… I think Zaar Aza just died."

She could barely speak the words before the tears took over.

"I'll be right there," he said, gently.

Two hours later, Paul arrived with Dan in tow. They laid Zaar Aza to rest in the back pasture with the others. The line of graves was growing—first the nameless mare from the grove, then Gabe, Gen, and the third horse that had arrived already gone. Next came Galaxy and Misha. And now, Zaar Aza.

Jenny stared at the markers, a lump rising in her throat. She turned to Paul.

"I don't know what I'm doing here anymore," she said, her voice breaking. "What's the point of all this? These animals come to me… and they just die."

Paul took her hands and squeezed them gently.

"Jenny, don't think of it that way," he said softly. "Yin and Yang didn't die; they are living their very best life. Johnnie Walker is safe and thriving because of you. And Happy is still here, isn't he?

"As for the ones who don't make it, you gave them love, dignity, and peace in their final days. That matters. It matters more than you know."

She didn't respond. Maybe she couldn't. Instead, she let herself lean into the silence as they walked back toward the house, together.

~ ~ * ~ ~

A few days later, Tristan was in the barn, quietly preparing Happy's dinner. The routine had become second nature by now—Jenny handled breakfast, turned Happy out (though he rarely ventured far these days), and Tristan came by in the afternoons to clean stalls, scrub buckets, refill water, and prep the evening feed.

With only Happy left, things had settled into a quieter rhythm. The old gelding didn't like being in the pasture alone—especially with winter creeping in—so Jenny had taken to opening all the stall doors, letting him wander the barn like a slow-moving king surveying his domain.

Jenny stepped softly into the feed room, leaning against the edge of a table behind Tristan.

"Hey, cowboy," she said with a grin.

"Hay yourself," he quipped, spinning around and tossing a small clump of hay in her direction.

She laughed and brushed it off her shoulder.

Tristan hesitated, suddenly a little fidgety. He glanced down at the scoop of feed in his hand, then back up at her. "Jenny, I wanted to ask you something."

Her eyebrows lifted in playful suspicion. "Uh-oh."

He shifted his weight, suddenly looking very un-Hollywood and very much like a guy about to ask a high school crush to prom. "So, I heard there's this big Cowboy Gala happening in December. Dinner, dancing, fundraising—for the animals and all that."

Jenny smirked. "Mmm, yes… I may have heard something about it."

He nodded, eyes dropping to his boots. "I was wondering if… maybe you'd want to go with me? As my date?"

For a moment, she said nothing.

Then Jenny crossed the short space between them, wrapped her arms around his waist, and pulled him close. Her kiss was slow, deep, and warm—filled with an answer that needed no words.

When she finally pulled away, her lips still brushing his, she smiled. "That answer your question?"

Tristan grinned, a little dazed. "Loud and clear."

From the other end of the barn, Happy gave a low, judgmental snort.

Jenny chuckled. "We'll take that as approval."

~ 22 ~
New Orleans Revisited
August 29, 2028

Six months before Uncle Brian passed, a business trip brought him back to New Orleans. As he walked through the airport, an uneasy feeling settled over him—like déjà vu with sharp edges. He couldn't quite place it, but it weighed on him.

He'd missed his flight—just barely. A major accident had shut down the freeway, and the pilot, indifferent to delays, had taken off right on time. So, Brian found himself waiting for the next flight home, hoping for a stand-by seat and trying to shake the gnawing sense of unease in his gut.

Thinking a drink might help, he wandered through the terminal and found the business class lounge. Brenda, the office manager at Ritter Bros. Construction, had signed them up for mileage rewards years ago, and for once, Brian was grateful for the foresight. He took a seat at the bar, ordered something strong, and tried to relax.

By his third drink, a man slid onto the stool beside him. Something about him made the hairs on Brian's neck stand. When the man spoke to the bartender, the sound of his voice unlocked a memory like a key in a long-forgotten door.

Brian turned. "Paul, right?"

The man looked over. "Paul Sr., actually. Do I know you?"

"Maybe your memory's not what it used to be," Brian said with a friendly smirk. "We met about twenty years ago. I'm Brian Ritter—Ritter Brothers Construction. My salesman Josh couldn't make the meeting, so I came in his place."

Recognition dawned on Paul's face. "Right. Yeah... I remember now. How are you?"

It was a polite enough question, but Brian could tell Paul didn't really care. His eyes were tired, his body language guarded. The man wasn't in the mood for small talk.

"I'm fine. You?"

Paul downed his drink in one gulp and signaled for another. "Not so good."

Brian leaned on the bar. "If you need someone to talk to, I've got nothing but time. Missed my flight, next one's in six hours."

Paul nodded his thanks, then ordered two drinks—one for himself, one for Brian.

"I just lost my job. Three hours ago." He let out a bitter laugh. "They moved me to a new department with some young manager, eager to use his newly gained power. He had it out for me from day one. I asked for this weekend off—told him it was important, family-related. He said no. Some policy about not taking time off until you've been in the position for 90 days. I reminded him I've been with the company 12 years. Didn't matter. He wanted me gone. I didn't show up this morning, and he left me a voicemail: Don't come back on Monday."

"Aren't you the owner? Don't you own Payne Lumber Company?" Brian asked.

"I was, I did. I lost the company about 5 years after you and I met," Paul answered.

Brian's brow furrowed. "What could be so important that you'd risk your current job?"

Paul didn't need to hear the question. He saw it on Brian's face.

"I come here every year," he said, voice quiet now. "Every year on this day. I come to look for my daughter." His eyes shimmered. "She disappeared here… twenty years ago. Same weekend you and I met, actually."

Brian's breath caught in his throat.

"I brought my family along on what was supposed to be a simple business trip. We thought we'd make it a little vacation. But Katrina was coming—we didn't know. If I'd known, I would've never brought them. It was my kids' third birthday."

He gave a hollow chuckle. "She was three years old. Her twin brother, my wife, and I—we were all here, trying to make the best of it. But during the chaos, the packing, the evacuation… we lost track of her. She vanished. Just swept away in the confusion."

He paused to gather himself. A guilty memory pounded in his heart.

"We searched everywhere. Superdome. Shelters. The streets. You'd think a three-year-old girl on her own would stand out. That someone would remember seeing her. But nothing. Every year we came back, hoping this would be the year we'd find her."

He drained another glass and set it down gently.

"My wife, Tala... said it felt like attending her funeral every year. We drained our savings, took out mortgages for investigators and travel expenses. Tala died of cancer a few years back. Maybe it's better she didn't see me lose the house last month. Between her treatment bills and the recession... it was too much. But she always said we had to stay, just in case our daughter ever came home."

Brian was quiet. His chest ached for the man beside him.

"What was her name?" he asked softly.

"Virginia," Paul said, his voice breaking. "But we called her Ginny."

~ 23 ~

Beechland Best Friends Gala

December, 2029

Tristan was all business that night—or at least he tried to be. He walked up to Jenny's front door, rang the bell, and took a steadying breath.

When she opened it, his composure evaporated.

"Whoa," he breathed, eyes widening. "You look…"

Jenny twirled once, her simple white lace dress catching the porch light. It slipped off one shoulder just so, paired perfectly with her favorite red cowboy boots—and of course, the matching red hat that made her look like a country music queen and rodeo star all at once.

"You clean up alright yourself," she said, eyeing his outfit. His flannel shirt was crisply pressed, Wranglers tight in that unmistakably Western way, polished Ariats on his feet, and a gleaming rodeo belt buckle front and center.

"Where did *that* come from?" she asked, pointing at the buckle.

Tristan gave a crooked grin. "My younger brother used to ride in the circuit. He lent it to me—thought I should show up with some credibility."

"Well," Jenny said with a teasing smile, slipping her hand into the crook of his arm, "you're practically legit now."

They pulled into the gala fashionably late—just as the welcome speeches had ended and the dinner service began. Tristan parked his truck along the edge of the lit driveway, and together they stepped into the barn, now transformed into a dreamscape.

Thousands of tiny lights shimmered from every beam and rafter, wrapping the space in a warm, magical glow. Tables were lined with auction items, each sparkling under strings of fairy lights. A soft buzz of conversation filled the air, blending with laughter and the clink of wine glasses.

Inside, Paul and Mary waved them over to a table near the front—just to the right of the stage, close enough to see everything, but not blocking anyone's view.

As Jenny took her seat, Tristan pulled out her chair like a gentleman, then leaned in for a kiss. "Be right back," he whispered. "This cowboy's gotta take a detour."

She smirked. "Better hurry. You'll miss the slideshow."

As he walked off, a few women nearby not-so-subtly tracked his departure, whispering behind napkins and wine glasses. Jenny just smiled to herself, adjusting her hat.

When Tristan returned, he slid back into his seat beside her and reached for her hand beneath the table. His other arm stretched behind her chair, fingers brushing her shoulder lightly.

That single movement drew a soft, audible sigh from a group of nearby women. Jenny didn't even look—she just smiled wider.

The projector flickered to life, casting a montage of rescue stories across a large screen: horses being led into clean stalls for the first time, emaciated dogs now bounding with joy, kittens curled in soft beds, owls and foxes blinking against the light of second chances. Volunteers smiled and waved. Familiar faces filled the screen.

Jenny felt Tristan's thumb brush her knuckles gently. She leaned into his side.

Conversation buzzed at their table as dinner was served— perfectly grilled steak, roasted vegetables, and crusty bread. The wine flowed, and laughter came easily. Mary and Paul, sitting side by side, looked unusually flushed.

Jenny raised an eyebrow at Mary, who gave her a mischievous smile.

"Oh," Paul said, trying to sound casual. "Guess tonight's as good a time as any—we're sort of... seeing each other."

Jenny and Tristan blinked at them in unison.

"Sort of?" Jenny echoed, laughing. "You're at a gala *together*, at the same table as us, and you coordinated outfits."

Mary grinned. "Fine. We're official. Now eat your dinner."

The night unfolded like something out of a country fairytale—good food, good people, soft light and laughter. And as Jenny sat there, her hand in Tristan's, hearts full all around her, she realized: the barn might've been quieter these days, but her life was anything but empty.

After the plates were cleared and coffee cups clinked onto saucers, a buzz of anticipation filled the barn. Jenny leaned over to Tristan with a smirk.

"Ready for the real rodeo?" He raised a brow. "Dessert?" She nodded. "Dessert dash. It's a full-contact sport."

At the front, a long table had been arranged with a dazzling spread of sweets: mile-high chocolate layer cake, lemon bars dusted with powdered sugar, pies of every variety, cupcakes stacked like monuments to frosting. Each table had bid in secret to earn first pick, and the top tables would have one member sprint to the dessert table—literally.

When their table was called—fifth place—Paul stood up, cracked his neck theatrically, and jogged in place.

"I've trained for this," he said solemnly, then bolted when the announcer gave the word.

The barn roared with laughter and applause. Paul weaved between tables like an Olympic hopeful, snagging a triple-berry cobbler and a whole platter of cookies before jogging back triumphantly.

"He takes pastries way too seriously," Mary whispered, beaming.

As guests savored their desserts and wiped away laughter tears, the raffle began.

A local radio personality took the mic, calling numbers with a dramatic flair. Jenny sat on the edge of her seat as prizes rolled by—gift baskets, spa packages, even a mini-vacation to a nearby mountain lodge. Of course, Paul won twice. And of course, he gifted one to Mary with a sheepish grin.

Jenny didn't win, but Tristan did—a free month of stall cleaning services from a local teen 4-H group.

"Looks like I'll be putting my boots up for a while," he teased.

"I'll believe it when I see it," Jenny shot back.

Once the last gift basket had been claimed, the real excitement of the evening kicked off. This year marked the 10th anniversary of the Beechland Best Friends Gala, and to celebrate, ten premium silent auction items had been donated— each one more extravagant than the last.

Jenny glanced at the brochure sitting neatly at the center of their table. "We didn't even get to see the auction items," she said with a shrug. "But I guess watching is just as fun."

Each item was described in detail—its real-world retail value listed beneath in bold type to emphasize just how generous these donations were. The auctioneer took the stage and began with the lowest-value item, working upward to build suspense.

The first prize was a $500 gift certificate to the local tack and feed store. The auctioneer worked the room like a seasoned showman, strolling the certificate across the stage like it was a treasure map. Then he drew a dramatic breath.

"And the highest bidder is... Tristan Clay, with a bid of $2,000!"

A mild ripple of applause ran through the barn. Tristan rose from his seat and ambled toward the stage. Jenny blinked in confusion. *Wait… what?*

Tristan leaned in and asked the auctioneer for the mic. "Sir," he began once the applause settled, "could you tell us who the second-highest bidder was?"

The auctioneer glanced at his sheet. "Esa Hartly."

Tristan smiled. "Esa, I'd like to re-gift this to you. Come on up and claim it."

A surprised squeal came from the back of the barn. A teenage girl—barely fifteen—rushed toward the stage and threw her arms around Tristan. The audience chuckled and clapped a little louder.

Jenny was still watching with her mouth slightly open when the second item was announced: two weeks of professional dog training lessons, valued at $800.

"And the winning bid of $2,500 goes to… Tristan Clay!"

The applause grew louder, mingled now with scattered whistles.

Again, Tristan took the mic. "Mikah Cooley, you were the second highest?" he asked, smiling toward the auctioneer. When Mikah's name was confirmed, Tristan announced, "then it's yours."

From that point on, the crowd's vibe shifted dramatically. What started as a few Karen-types muttering about a rich Hollywood actor "buying the whole table" turned into full-on cheers and celebratory shouts as the pattern continued.

Item after item, Tristan's name was called. Each time, Tristan double or triple bid what the item was worth.

A custom saddle worth $3,500—Tristan won it, then gifted it to a young barrel racer.

A winery carriage tour—Tristan again. "Terry Phillips?" he asked into the mic. A resounding "YES!" came from the left side of the barn and a blond woman came running up to the stage.

A private tour of the Wild Cat Sanctuary in Norfolk—Tristan won and passed it on to a local vet tech. Carrie Mannon had bid three times and lost out each time. She was sitting in the middle of the barn, quietly resigned to the fact that she hadn't won the tour. When her name was called, she missed it the first time around. "Carrie Mannon?" Tristan asked again, "anyone know her?" Someone at her table gave her a nudge, as she couldn't believe she won.

A weekend getaway in Cancun—yep, Tristan again. "Jackie Lodds, come on up!" Tristan called. This went to a lovely lady with long beautiful silver hair, braided perfectly down her back. "My husband and I can finally go on our honeymoon!" she squealed.

From her seat, Jenny began piecing it together. When he'd excused himself earlier, it wasn't for the "little cowboy's room" at all — he had slipped away to place bids on every single auction item. Her heart clenched, unexpectedly. *When did I start underestimating him so much?*

The crowd was wild with excitement by the time the final item was announced: a one-week cruise from Virginia to Maine during peak fall foliage, valued at $6,500.

"And the final highest bid," the auctioneer called, voice shaking slightly from emotion, "is $15,000—once again, from Tristan Clay!"

The barn erupted. No polite clapping now—just stomping boots, whoops, and hollers.

Tristan stepped onto the stage one last time, but this time he leaned in so only the auctioneer could hear. "Who has the second highest bidder?"

"April Atkins," the auctioneer whispered back.

Tristan raised the mic. "I hope you don't mind, but I'm going to keep this one for myself."

The crowd gasped, a few chuckles mixed with disappointed murmurs.

"But…" he continued, turning to the back, "April Atkins—would you come up to the stage please?"

A lovely woman made her way slowly through the tables, cheeks pink.

"April," Tristan said gently, "you were the second-highest bidder. I hope it's alright, but I'd like to buy another identical cruise and give it to you."

For a breathless second, the barn went silent.

Then it *exploded.*

Chairs scraped back as the crowd jumped to their feet, cheering, clapping, whistling—pure, unfiltered joy. April's hand flew to her mouth, and she hugged Tristan like someone who just got the best surprise of her life.

Another eruption of applause shook the walls.

After the last silent auction item had been claimed, the energy in the barn still buzzed with laughter, applause, and the occasional joyful tear. But before the band could strike up their first note, Tristan stepped back up onto the stage and gestured for the microphone once more.

The room quieted quickly.

He looked out across the sea of faces — volunteers in denim and barn boots, families with muddy pickup trucks parked outside, and wide-eyed teens still beaming from their raffle wins. He took a deep breath and spoke:

"I only play a hero in the movies," he began, voice steady, humble. "But you guys — you're the real heroes."

A murmur of appreciation ran through the crowd.

"You're out there every single day — rescuing, rehabbing, nursing the broken, the abandoned, the neglected, speaking up for the voiceless — just because it's the right thing to do. You don't get standing ovations or red carpets. You get 4 a.m. feedings, frostbitten fingers, and mud on your good jeans."

A few laughs rippled through the crowd.

"I've never met such selfless people in my life. And I just want you to know... I see you. All of you. And I'm honored — truly honored — to be a small part of this tonight. My only hope is that I can live up to your example and maybe do a little good in this world too."

There was a still moment — soft, reverent silence — and then the entire barn erupted into cheers, louder than any applause yet that night. People rose to their feet, clapping, whistling, even stamping their boots.

Jenny, watching from her seat, felt a swell of pride so strong it brought tears to her eyes. Not because he was famous, or generous, or wearing that ridiculous belt buckle. But because, in a barn full of people who gave everything for animals that had nothing, he'd found a way to belong.

And in her heart, she knew — he already did.

Jenny just sat there, stunned, while the barn lit up with noise. Tristan returned to the table, humble and quiet, sliding into his seat like he hadn't just rewritten the rules of generosity. He reached for her hand under the table.

"You okay?" he asked, a bit bashful.

She nodded, swallowing the lump in her throat. "You … you're incredible."

He shrugged. "Just trying to keep up with you."

Before she could say more, the auctioneer spoke again.

The auctioneer took the mic again, blinking rapidly. "Well, folks, I've never seen anything like this in all my years doing this event. With all ten items combined, the total raised for tonight's silent auction is… $61,700! Combine that with the dessert dash, the dinner tickets and the raffle, the total money raised tonight came to…" a drumroll of stomping boots and hands on tables erupted, "$101,052!" And the crowd came out of their chairs. "Folks, I'm told that the most we've raised to date."

Once the roar of the crown dissipated, and the last round of applause echoed through the rafter, the auctioneer announced, "Well, folks," he said, still holding back a grin, "now that our wallets are lighter and our hearts are full, it's time for the best part of the evening – the **barn dance**! Y'all know what to do!"

He waved a hand toward the crowd. "Grab your chairs and tables and scoot 'em to the sides. Let's uncover that dance floor—we've got some boots that need dusting!"

There was a cheerful commotion as chairs scraped back and guests grabbed the corners of tables, sliding them toward the barn's edges. Beneath the rearranged furniture, the polished wooden floor gleamed under strings of fairy lights—clearly prepped for just this moment.

Jenny and Tristan helped push their table aside, laughing as one of the centerpieces nearly toppled.

The lights dimmed slightly, and a country band struck up its first chords. Boots tapped, laughter echoed, and chairs scraped across the old wooden floors as everyone made way for the dance floor.

Jenny looked at Tristan and held out her hand.

"You ready for this?" Jenny asked, raising an eyebrow.

Tristan gave a crooked grin. "Born ready."

"Cowboy," she said, "you owe me a dance."

He grinned. "I'm all yours."

The band in the corner—a five-piece country group with fiddles and a steel guitar—kicked off with a twangy two-step. Couples spilled into the center of the barn, laughter rising as cowboy hats tilted and boots began to stomp in rhythm.

Tristan took Jenny's hand and spun her toward him. She landed with a small squeal and a laugh against his chest, and he immediately took the lead, guiding her into a slow, easy sway.

"You're not half bad," she teased.

"I've seen Footloose at least five times," he said. "I know things."

They moved together effortlessly, her red boots stepping lightly across the floor, his arms firm and steady around her. The music shifted to a faster tempo, and he spun her out, then back in, making her laugh as her hat nearly flew off.

Around them, friends old and new danced—Mary and Paul side-stepping with surprising rhythm, volunteers twirling each other like they'd been practicing for weeks.

When the band slowed the pace, playing a sweet country ballad, Tristan pulled Jenny closer. They swayed in the center of the floor, his hands resting on the small of her back, hers around his neck.

"This is perfect," he said quietly, forehead resting against hers.

"It really is," she whispered back.

In that moment, with the scent of hay and candlewax in the air, the glow of lights above them, and laughter echoing all around, Jenny realized this wasn't just a celebration—it was a turning point. A beginning.

One she hadn't even known she was waiting for.

~ 24 ~
Happiness is Relative

December, 2029

The empty barn took a toll on Happy. Each morning when Jenny opened his stall to let him into the pasture, he refused to move. To him, it was just a larger space to feel alone in. Concerned, Jenny called Mary to ask if any horses needed fostering, but there were none at the moment.

Without a companion, Happy began to decline. He seemed withdrawn, stiff-legged, and reluctant to leave his stall. Jenny shared her worries with Paul over the phone, and he suggested arthritis and loneliness were to blame. He recommended putting a mirror in Happy's stall, saying it might make him feel less alone. Jenny was doubtful. Happy was too clever to be fooled by a reflection.

And, just as she suspected, the mirror didn't help.

Over the next few days, Happy's condition worsened. He stopped eating and grew lethargic. Then, one afternoon, while she and Tristan were reorganizing the tack room between shared kisses, a loud, unnatural thump echoed through the barn.

They rushed out. Happy wasn't in view.

They ran to his stall and found him collapsed on the floor, breathing heavily, his body convulsing. When the spasms subsided, they tried to coax him up, but he wouldn't—or couldn't—stand.

Paul arrived within twenty minutes, heading straight to the barn without stopping at the house. He began with his stethoscope, then ran practiced hands over Happy's frame. His touch paused near the hind leg.

"How long has he had this cut?" he asked. The wound looked minor, but the leg was swollen and radiating heat.

Jenny shook her head. "I didn't even know it was there."

Paul frowned, eyes heavy. "It's badly infected. I think he has tetanus. The stiffness, the lack of appetite, locked jaw—it all lines up. He's very sick, Jenny."

There was no blame in his voice, but guilt hit her like a weight. How had she missed this?

"I'll give him a strong dose of penicillin and the tetanus antitoxin," Paul said. "Monitor him closely. I'd stay, but I've got other animals to see. Call me if he worsens."

After administering the injections, the three of them worked to help Happy to his feet. Once he was stable, Paul left with a final word: "Keep me updated."

Jenny stayed by Happy's side all afternoon. Tristan stayed for a while but eventually had to leave. Alone now, Jenny watched over her friend. He stood in his stall, head low, unmoving, barely reacting to her presence.

She did everything she could. Cleaned his wound. Sponged him with cool water to bring down his fever. She even blended his grain into a warm mash and tried to syringe it past his clenched teeth, aiming for the gap where a bit would sit—but he refused to eat. He didn't fight her, but he had no will left.

As night fell, she stayed by his side, massaging his swollen joints. Jenny had read all about Reiki and massage and how it could help in all sorts of situations. She gave it a go. She started at his head, gently working in small circles down his neck, then moved to each leg, kneading the swollen, tight muscles from hoof to belly. Again and again, she worked four full circuits until she could hardly keep her eyes open.

There was nothing more to be done.

Utterly spent, she trudged back to the house and collapsed on the couch. She flipped on the switch for the gas fireplace, watching the colored flames flicker—blue, then red, then gold—reflecting off the glass and casting strange shadows on the wall.

Her gaze fell to the andiron set. It had always struck her as odd—an elaborate medieval knight holding a tall poker and a tiny coal shovel, guarding a fake fire. There were no coals to stir, no ashes to clean. Why had anyone ever bought such a thing?

Curious, she reached for the poker. It tipped and clanged to the floor with a metallic bang. Jenny rolled down to the floor, brushing her hand over the hardwood to check for scratches—when something white caught her eye beneath the couch.

A corner of paper. Dusty, forgotten.

She stretched her arm beneath the couch, shoulder straining, fingers just shy of reaching. Frustrated, she grabbed the fallen poker and carefully drew the object toward her. Dust bunnies clung to it as it slid across the floor.

It was an envelope. Thick with dust. Her heart skipped as she recognized the handwriting on the front.

It was from Uncle Brian. The front if it read:

My Dearest Jenny

After resetting the andiron on its base, Jenny sank back onto the couch, the envelope resting in her lap. She wiped away the thick layer of dust with her sleeve. It had been nearly a year since she'd last held it, but she knew exactly where it had come from—and what it contained. Even though she'd never opened it, the weight of it in her hands stirred old memories and unspoken fears.

She turned it over slowly, running her thumb along the sealed flap. Just as she slipped her finger into the fold, a loud honk echoed from the driveway.

Paul.

He'd come to check on Happy one more time before heading home. Jenny quickly stuffed the envelope into her coat pocket, hoping—desperately—that Paul had brought some kind of his Indian woo-woo magic with him.

Inside the barn, Paul ran through his routine: stethoscope to chest, hands gliding over Happy's frame, checking the wound. He asked Jenny for the timing of the doses she'd given, nodding thoughtfully as she answered. Together, they managed to coax Happy to his feet once more.

Paul stepped back, his expression unreadable. "There's really not much more we can do now. The syringe feeding—

good thinking, even if he's not eating. He just feels awful. But keep at it. You might catch him on a better moment."

His tone was kind, encouraging—but Jenny didn't feel encouraged. She nodded, trying to absorb the compliment, but inside, she felt hollow. Like she had failed him.

After Paul left, she locked up the barn, trudged back to the house, and slipped into her warmest flannel pajamas. Sleep claimed her the moment her head hit the pillow; the weight of the envelope still tucked away in her coat pocket—and the worry for Happy pressing heavy on her heart.

~ ~ * ~ ~

The weather reports said that snow was coming that night, but that it would be mild, a few stray flakes here and there. She awoke to eight inches of snow. *A few flakes my ass! Damn weatherman never gets anything right!* She checked on Happy, he was again lying down in his stall. She hoped the medicine had helped as she started the drive towards town, reminding herself to call Paul once she got there.

By the time she was able to leave, there was already another inch added to the previous nights' eight inches on the ground, and it just got thicker and harder the closer she got to Beechland. The drive was slow; the normal 30-minute trip took 55 minutes. She needed to get everything on her list before the snow became any worse, but she didn't want to slide off the road due to the ice.

As she drove into town, the snow subsided a bit. The snowflakes were small, and falling lazily in the air, whipping around before gravity took hold.

She did her grocery shopping quickly and placed the items in the backseat of her truck. They would be safe there. Just as she was leaving, she received a call from Paul, so she hopped in the truck to better hear the conversation; the wind was starting to whip up again.

"Jenny, it's Paul." She thought it funny that he still felt the need to announce who was calling. "I have to go out to Ocracoke Island out on the Banks. We got a report of a horse that's wounded and isn't doing so well. Maybe I can bring it over and we can watch it over at your place. It might help Happy recover quicker. Mind if I take Tristan with me?"

"Not at all, help yourself." She laughed at that, knowing how she wasn't technically his boss. She heard her phone beep, low battery.

"Ok, truth time, I'm already here. Tristan's hooking up your trailer as we speak, I just didn't want you to panic when you saw his truck, and he wasn't around." Jenny could hear him chuckle with a note of apology. "I also checked on Happy, he's not doing any better, but keep up the faith, it takes a while for tetanus to work its way out of the blood stream."

"Thanks Paul. I appreciate your little pep talk. Oh, and be really careful, it's pretty dicey out there," and her phone went dead.

"Sure thing… Mom." He laughed and hung up, not even aware that she was already off the line.

She opened the truck door and was assaulted by the stinging cold, the small flakes falling even quicker than before. She had one last stop to make before heading back home to help with Happy; she needed her coffee. She trudged her way to Dannie's Diner, pushing against the wind and the snow freezing her face. As she entered the diner, she stomped her boots to loosen any snow that had accumulated.

The diner was overflowing with customers, new and old, all taking shelter against the weather outside. Booths were filling up quickly; strangers introduced themselves, and old friends were reacquainted, seats were disappearing. Jenny saw one last empty seat in a booth to the rear of the right side, all the way to the back, so close to the kitchen the smells overpowered her senses.

Jenny found herself standing across from the Sheriff and two deputies of Hyde County. Sheriff Sawyer introduced himself and asked before sitting. He was fit for a 50+ year old, his white hair a stark contrast with his dark skin and gray eyes. Jenny noted how gray eyes seemed to be a common trait in the region.

"So, Jenny… how goes the horse healing?"

"Um, what?" Jenny was confused not only how he knew her, but also what she did.

"It's a small town, everyone knows everything," he apologized.

Jenny was comforted and thought it a good thing he knew what she did and where she was; if there were any problems she could count on him. She shrugged off her coat and noticed the letter she had put in the pocket the day before.

"It's all well, although I may have a problem getting back home with this snow," she replied.

The snow was falling even harder then, the flakes growing large, full and fluffy, and the wind was brutally growling, the white-out conditions kept anyone from leaving the diner.

Dannie's staff had all made it in, with the exception of one of the two cooks. Dannie and two waitresses worked like clockwork; one person starting from the far right, one from the far left, and one at the counter. The first thing they all did was bring coffee to all patrons in order, starting at the far ends and meeting in the middle. Then they started taking orders in the same manner.

Every four orders, each waitress brought the sheet to the cook, and from then on it was like watching a well-choreographed ballet. The waitresses would drop off the ticket, a few moments later the cook would yell, "Order Up! Order Up! Order Up! Order Up!" It reminded Jenny of the SNL skit with John Belushi taking orders in a diner much like *Dannie's*, then yelling the order to the kitchen. "Cheeseburger, cheeseburger, cheeseburger, cheeseburger, no fries, no coke! We have Pepsi, we have chips!" Then Dan Ackroyd on the grill repeated the order, "Cheeseburger, cheeseburger, cheeseburger, cheeseburger, one Pepsi, one chips!" Jenny couldn't help but crack a little chuckle.

As the platefuls reached the tables, the roar of the crowd trying to yell over everyone else to hear each other's conversations quickly quieted down and was replaced with the clinking of silverware and coffee mugs. The snow was falling harder and harder. All eyes turned towards the windows.

Jenny took the quiet of the diner as an opportunity to read the letter. She sat back into the booth and opened the envelope. She unfolded three hand-written pages:

My Dearest Jenny,

I know this is quite a shock, but for once I wanted to do something right, even if I won't be around to see it. I know I wasn't always the best parent, but I did the best that I could. I'm sorry for not being honest with you up front, and I hope this makes up for it. And I hope it will answer any questions you may have about who you are.

When you were 3 years old, I found you in New Orleans, lost, cold and frightened, and away from your family. It was the day after Hurricane Katrina. I searched and searched for your family but could not find them. So, I decided to bring you home. I knew that Anna and Pete (your parents) wanted children, but couldn't have any, so I brought you to them. They called you their "little miracle". But it was still a secret we had to keep.

And then Anna and Pete died. I had many thoughts about what to do, what would be the right thing, but in the end, you were still my family. And I loved you as much as Pete and Anna did. So, I decided to give you the home you needed.

The truth is, your real family never stopped looking for you, even now, 23 years later. I didn't know it at the time, but I knew your real father. I did some business with him in New Orleans, right before Hurricane Katrina.

Then last year I saw him again in an airport. He had an interesting story to tell. He told me about his daughter that went missing years ago, after Hurricane Katrina. That child was, IS you.

The rest of your family gave up after ten years of searching and finally let go. They even had a funeral. But every year on that anniversary your father would fly to New Orleans and look for you. He never stopped looking for you.

I knew right then and there that I had to make this right. But I couldn't tell him right out what I had done.

His name is Paul Payne, Sr. Your mother's name is Tala, and you have a twin brother, Paul, Jr. Your real name is Virginia; your family called you Ginny. You are from Beechland, VA.

Your father mentioned that over the years his luck had run out, and they had lost the family home. The house you are standing in now is that home, the home you grew up in, your home. I bought it from the bank to give it back to you and your family.

I hope you understand why I couldn't just tell you, why I had to send you here with a letter and a key. I am so ashamed of what I did. I thought I was helping. I thought I was giving you a second chance, when in reality I took you from your true family.

I can only hope that by reuniting you with your family that you can one day forgive me for what I've done. I do love you very much Jenny.

All My Love,
Uncle Brian

Jenny let out a breath she didn't realize she'd been holding. Her mind raced. Too much at once—too much to absorb. *I have a family. A real family. This is my home. I have a brother...* Her eyes widened. *Holy crap—PAUL is my brother!*

She grabbed her phone to call him, but it was dead. She needed to get home to use the landline.

Across the table, Sheriff Sawyer's radio crackled to life. "Well," he said, rising from the table, "that's my cue. Accident on Route 12."

The deputies stood with him, pulling on their coats. Sawyer reached for his wallet.

"Here," Jenny said, placing two twenties on the table. "Breakfast is on me."

The men hesitated, surprised.

"Jenny, we can't accept gratuities," the sheriff replied, raising a hand.

"With all due respect, Sheriff, you've got an accident to get to. Please—just go."

She smiled at him, gently but firmly. Her gratitude was sincere.

The three officers exchanged glances, then nodded their thanks, grabbed their hats, and left. The bell above the door jingled as they stepped into the snow.

Route 12 was on her way home. She didn't hesitate. Slipping out behind them, she braced herself against the biting wind and climbed into her truck. The snow was coming down harder now, thick and blinding. She followed the red and blue lights through the storm, careful to stay far enough back to avoid scolding but close enough not to lose her path. Their slow crawl at twenty miles an hour meant the drive home would take at least an hour.

Fifteen miles from her house, the patrol cars came to a halt. Jenny eased her truck to a stop and peered through the windshield. Visibility was poor, but she could make out the shape of a pickup truck, twisted and tilted across the road into a ditch, the front end mangled, the roof caved in. One headlight still burned weakly; the other was shattered.

But what froze the blood in her veins was the horse trailer hitched behind it—or rather, no longer hitched. It had come free during the crash, landing in the ditch on the other side of the road. Her heart pounded.

She wasn't a praying woman, but in that moment, she bowed her head and begged whatever god might be listening: *Please let the horse be okay.*

She jumped out, slipping slightly on the icy shoulder, and made her way toward the wreck. Sheriff Sawyer stepped in front of her, arm outstretched.

"I can help," she said, louder than she meant to, pointing to the trailer. He paused, then nodded and stepped aside.

Jenny made her way to the trailer, half-sliding down the snowy embankment. Her hand caught the side to steady herself. She was covered in snow, but didn't care. She yanked onto the trailer door, praying it was empty.

It was.

A wave of relief swept over her. She leaned against the trailer, catching her breath.

Then—a noise. Faint, distant. A shuffling. A moan.

She turned toward the sound, crossing the road as carefully as she could. There, she saw it: a trail of hoofprints in the snow. On the opposite side of the road, long skid marks scarred the surface. The truck had swerved to avoid something and lost control.

Jenny followed the sound, trudging through the snow until she found it.

A deer.

A full-grown buck, antlers short but proud. He was sprawled in the brush, sides heaving, blood trickling from his mouth and one ear.

Jenny slipped down the ditch again, then climbed up to where he lay. Slowly, she lowered herself beside him and cradled his head in her lap. His fur was thick with winter, tawny and soft beneath her hands. His tail was white underneath, black-tufted on top.

And then the world dimmed. The flashing lights dulled into pale whites. His fur turned gray, his color draining like breath from a lung.

"Shshsh," she whispered, stroking his neck. "It's okay."

His legs stilled. His breathing slowed. His eyes met hers—full of pain, then peace.

"Shshsh," she repeated softly. "It's okay. You're safe. You're free"

She sat with him as his life ebbed away. Death had come again, as it so often did. She wondered if it would ever stop—if she would ever stop bearing witness to these final moments.

When the deer was gone, she held him a moment longer. Slowly, the world brightened again. The colors crept back. She gently laid his head in the snow, smoothed the fur behind his ear, and gave a final pat.

"See you on the other side," she murmured, then stood and walked back through the falling snow.

Jenny scrambled back across the ditch, her boots slipping on the ice as she climbed toward the wreck. The flashing red and blue lights pulsed against the snow, disorienting her vision. As she neared the passenger side of the truck, she saw why Sheriff Sawyer had tried to stop her.

Tristan.

His head was slumped against the shattered window, streaked with blood. A low gasp escaped her lips. She reached through the broken glass and touched his shoulder, her voice shaking.

"Tristan? Tristan!"

He stirred, slowly raising his right arm to his head. His eyes blinked open, unfocused.

"I'm okay," he mumbled. "Just a scratch." He gave a weak chuckle and winced. "Paul? You okay, buddy?"

No response.

"Paul?" he called again, louder this time. Still nothing.

Jenny's stomach dropped. She pushed herself around the front of the truck, slipping once before grabbing the hood to steady herself. Paul's side window had also shattered. His head lay motionless against the steering wheel.

The sounds of sirens and squawking radios echoed around her, merging into a deafening blur. Her mind flashed back to the night Galaxy died—those same frantic sounds, the same helpless feeling. Her stomach twisted.

With the help of a deputy, Jenny managed to force the driver's side door open. Paul collapsed into her arms as the door gave way, his body limp. They both fell into the snow.

"Paul!" she cried, cradling him. "Paul, wake up!"

She ripped off her gloves and pressed her fingers to his neck, searching desperately for a pulse. Nothing. She tried again, her hands trembling.

"Come on… please…" she whispered, shaking him, as if that alone might bring him back. "I need to tell you something! I need you not to die!" But he didn't respond. The white snow beneath him was turning red—thick trails of blood seeping from his body, staining everything.

Jenny sat in the snow, rocking back and forth, Paul in her arms. Her tears froze against her cheeks, the cold biting through her coat, her breath hitching with every sob.

Paramedics arrived, one carrying a backboard, the other already assessing the scene. Gently, they lifted Paul from her grasp and onto a littler and carried him up the ditch. Another EMT offered Jenny a hand, pulling her to her feet and helping her back to the road.

Tristan had already been secured to a stretcher and was being wheeled into an ambulance. Jenny stood there, shivering—not from the cold, but from shock. She couldn't move.

Sheriff Sawyer approached her, his voice soft. "Jenny, are you okay?"

She opened her mouth, but the words caught in her throat. "He's… he's my…"

"Jenny?" The sheriff rested his hand on her arm.

She looked at him, eyes wide and hollow. "He's my brother."

Sawyer's expression shifted, registering the weight of what she'd said. He gently guided her toward the ambulance where Paul had been loaded.

"Come on," he said. "You need to be with your family."

Jenny climbed inside without protesting, sinking into the seat beside Paul. Her hand found his, cold and unresponsive. As the doors closed behind her, the world outside faded into a blur of sirens and snow.

~ ~ * ~ ~

The wail of the siren blurred into the background, a steady, distant howl that barely registered over the rush of adrenaline in Jenny's veins. She sat on the bench seat in the back of the ambulance, gripping the edge of the gurney where Paul lay motionless, pale beneath the harsh fluorescent lights.

He looked so still.

Too still.

His hand—usually calloused and warm—felt cool in hers, his fingers limp and smudged with dirt and blood. A paramedic monitored his vitals nearby, calling out quiet updates Jenny barely heard.

Then, without warning, Paul's eyelids fluttered.

"Paul?" she breathed, leaning in. "JayJay!!"

His eyes cracked open, just a sliver, unfocused. He blinked slowly, like it took every ounce of strength he had.

"I need to tell you," Jenny whispered, brushing a strand of hair from his forehead. "Don't talk. Just listen."

He looked at her—really looked at her—for half a second. Confused. Lost.

So she gave him something to hold onto.

"You're my brother," she said softly, her voice steady despite the sting in her throat. "You hear me? I'm your GinGin! You found me!"

Paul's brow twitched—just enough to show he heard her. His lips moved slightly, trying to form words, "GinGin," he whispered, just barely loud enough for her to make it out. He had heard her. He understood! He remembered!

A tear slid down her cheek before she could stop it. She leaned closer, still holding his hand.

"You're not going anywhere. Not yet. You've got too many fence posts left to fix. And Snookie's going to pitch a fit if you miss another feeding."

His lips curved—barely, but it was there. A faint smile, or maybe just the ghost of one.

Then his eyes drifted closed again.

But this time, Jenny didn't panic. Because she knew he'd heard her. Knew it had landed somewhere deep, anchored in whatever strength he had left.

She squeezed his hand.

"You're my family," she whispered. "I'm finally home."

~ 25 ~

Crossing Over

December, 2029

Jenny sat alone in the sterile, fluorescent-lit waiting room, the cold from outside still clinging to her coat and boots. Her mind wandered, spiraling through memories of Galaxy—how he died in the snow, how helpless she had felt. The grief was fresh again, sharp and unrelenting.

Then a soft voice broke through the fog of her thoughts.

"My dear," it said gently.

Jenny turned, startled. Standing behind her was Paul's grandmother. No... *her* grandmother. Relief surged through her. She shot up from the hard plastic chair and wrapped her arms around the woman, burying her face in that familiar cloud of white hair.

"Grandma," she whispered, trying to choke back the sob rising in her throat. "I'm so glad you're here. But... how did you know?"

"The sheriff called me," her grandmother replied with a soft smile. "Small towns talk. News travels fast." She gestured to the seat beside her. "How are you holding up?"

Jenny sat, exhausted. "Honestly? Not great. I've been waiting for hours. No updates. No one will let me see Paul or

261

Tristan. But more than that... I found something out. Something important. I was going to tell Paul first, but..."

She hesitated, chewing her lip, unsure where to begin.

"Just tell me," Grandma said gently. "Whatever it is, I can take it."

Jenny searched her face. What if she didn't believe her? What if this all ended in another heartbreak?

"My real name," Jenny began quietly, "is Virginia. Virginia Payne. Ginny, for short."

She looked up, holding her breath.

Her grandmother didn't flinch. Instead, she smiled—warm and knowing. "I know, my dear. I knew the first moment I saw you."

Jenny blinked. "You... knew?"

"I did. But you didn't. I had to wait for *you* to see it. If I had said something too soon, it would have sounded like the ramblings of an old woman clinging to hope."

Jenny stared into her grandmother's eyes and, for the first time, noticed they were the exact same shade as her own.

"You're Paul's twin," Grandma said, reaching for her hand. "Which means... you have the gift."

"The gift?" Jenny echoed.

"Yes. Every pair of twins in our family line has it—one to heal the wounded – of flesh and soul. The other to guide the lost, walking between worlds to find their way. Paul's calling was to heal. That's why he became a vet. You, Jenny... you're the other half."

Jenny sat in stunned silence as pieces began snapping into place—memories, stories, the journals, the animals. The Civil War twins. The white buffalo. The grove behind her house.

All of it.

Her childhood pets hadn't died *because* of her. They had come *to* her. To be comforted. To be helped.

She let the realization settle like warm sunlight over frost.

"You alright, sweetheart?" Grandma asked, her hand warm and grounding.

Jenny looked at her, a slow smile spreading across her face. "Yeah. For the first time in a long time… I really am."

They sat together in the stillness, a quiet understanding between them. Then the doctor entered.

His face was solemn.

"I'm afraid we're still waiting for things to change," he said.

Jenny and Grandma stood at the same time, instinctively, like they were moving as one.

"Paul sustained a major head injury," the doctor continued. "He hit the window hard—there was significant trauma and extensive bleeding. We're doing everything in our power. He's in a coma; we're just waiting for him to regain consciousness."

Jenny stared at him, unblinking.

"I'm so sorry," he added softly. His voice cracked, but he didn't let the tears fall. "I'll come back when I have more news."

For a moment, nothing moved. Then Jenny turned away, stumbled to the corner of the room, and threw up into the wastebasket. Her body heaved, the grief crashing through her like a wave.

Her grandmother was there instantly, holding her hair back, rubbing gentle circles on her back. When Jenny finally straightened up, pale and trembling, she turned to the doctor.

"What about Tristan?" she asked hoarsely. "Do you know anything?"

"He's in surgery," the doctor said. "I'll have someone update you as soon as possible. I promise."

Jenny looked at her grandmother.

The doctor gave a respectful nod and left.

Jenny sat down again beside her grandmother. The tears had stopped, but her eyes were hollow. The weight of it all sat heavy in her chest.

"I just found my brother," she whispered. "I can't lose him again," she whispered.

Her grandmother took her hand. "You have family, Jenny. You have me."

Jenny leaned against her shoulder, and they sat quietly, waiting together in the cold, impersonal room—two survivors holding onto the only thing left that mattered. Each other.

"Grandmother?" Jenny asked softly, the word catching on the edge of awe. "If *you're* a direct descendant of Virginia Dare… that means *I* am too, doesn't it?"

Niskadi nodded, her smile gentle, eyes shining with the weight of shared legacy.

Jenny stood still, letting the truth wash over her. The bloodline. The gifts. The echoes of the past woven into her own story. It all made sense now—why she could feel things, *know* things.

This wasn't just history. It was *hers*.

She pressed a hand to her heart, her thoughts jumping to Tristan. He had to pull through. He *had* to.

Because she couldn't wait to tell him.

~ ~ * ~ ~

Several more hours crawled by. Jenny's nausea returned in relentless waves, sending her back and forth to the bathroom every half hour. Eventually, a kind nurse noticed and offered her something for the sickness. The anti-nausea meds finally gave her a small reprieve.

She sat curled beside her grandmother, both of them suspended in a fog of grief and waiting. The hospital's air was dry, the chairs uncomfortable, but Jenny barely noticed. Her thoughts looped endlessly, circling around everything that had happened since the accident.

"Grandma," she asked quietly, "are my parents still alive?"

Her grandmother didn't answer right away. She looked at Jenny with soft, apologetic eyes. "No, sweetheart. They both passed not long ago. It's just us now."

Jenny let that settle over her, a quiet ache spreading in her chest.

She glanced at her grandmother again. "So... if Paul doesn't make it, what happens to the gift? There's always supposed to be two, right? One who heals, one who guides. What happens if it's just me?"

Her grandmother reached for her hand, gave it a gentle squeeze. "Mother Earth has a way of restoring balance. I don't know what form that will take—but I believe you're exactly where you're meant to be." Her eyes sparkled faintly, the corners creased with a knowing smile. "Just be ready."

Jenny didn't say a word. She turned and rushed down the hallway, back into the bathroom, where she collapsed over the sink and retched again—expelling the remnants of vending machine snacks and the last remnants of hope in her gut.

She stayed hunched there for a long time, the cold porcelain against her hands grounding her as her world tilted, yet again.

~ ~ * ~ ~

When Jenny finally returned home after the endless day at the hospital, she didn't even stop to take off her coat. She went straight to the barn.

Happy was still lying in his stall, his breathing slow and shallow. Jenny sank to the ground beside him, gently lifting his head into her lap. She bent forward, burying her face in his tangled mane, and wept—quiet, aching sobs that soaked into his fur.

As the grief of the unknown poured out of her, something strange and wonderful stirred in the air. A warmth radiated around her, curling around her body like an embrace. Her skin tingled. A soft, brilliant light filled the stall, shimmering across Happy's coat. Jenny opened her eyes.

Happy's white fur glowed with an ethereal light, refracting into every color of the rainbow. He looked almost... otherworldly. Alive in a way she couldn't explain. Jenny blinked, sure it was just exhaustion playing tricks on her. She closed her eyes again and let the tears flow.

Eventually, she fell asleep with his head still resting in her lap.

At 6 a.m., she was jolted awake by the sound of movement, Happy was stirring. She scrambled to her feet and moved aside, watching him attempt to rise. He rocked forward, his limbs shaky, and after a few tries—he stood. Jenny gasped.

His fever was gone. His body no longer radiated heat. He dipped his head and drank deeply from the water bucket, sucking the water in through his teeth, then nudged his empty grain pail expectantly.

Jenny rushed back to the kitchen and made a fresh mash of soaked grain, no longer needing the syringe to feed him. When she returned, Happy eagerly devoured every bite. He was alert. He was eating. He was healing.

For the first time she could remember, an animal had recovered under her care—not died. And it hadn't been luck. It had been her.

A deep, quiet sense of awe filled her chest. But it was quickly followed by the heavy weight of unsurety. Paul was in the hospital. Tristan was in the hospital. The joy of Happy's recovery was fleeting. She didn't know how to live in this new silence, without either of them.

A month passed. Happy had fully healed, his strength returned. But without Galaxy, he was different—quieter, more withdrawn. Mary had found a peaceful sanctuary for blind horses, a place where Happy could live out his days in calm, secure companionship. Jenny knew it was the right decision.

The day he left, she stood in the doorway of the empty barn. For the first time since she arrived, it was silent. Still.

It had been a year since she left Boston, carrying nothing but a key inside an envelope. One year that changed everything. And standing there now, alone but transformed, she knew this wasn't the end. It was the beginning of something new.

Once again, she was all alone, until she wasn't.

~ Epilogue ~
Beechland Equine Rescue

Three months later, Jenny made her usual morning walk to the barn, the wooden boards creaking beneath her boots like a familiar song. Though the stalls had long since been cleaned and empty, she moved through them one by one—refluffing already fresh shavings, scrubbing water buckets that didn't need it, hanging them to dry with unnecessary care. Rituals, really. Things to keep her hands busy while her heart caught up.

The silence inside pressed down like snow—soft, but heavy. Without hoofbeats or the rustle of hay, even her breath sounded too loud. No nickers, no impatient pawing at the stall doors. Just stillness.

She paused at Galaxy's stall, letting her fingers graze the smooth grain of the wood. The memories were still here, tucked into the corners like sunlight that refused to fade Misha's sleeping on Galaxy. Tristan's lopsided grin. Paul's corny jokes. Yin and Yang being their opposite, but true selves. All that chaos. All that love.

Her hand dropped to her belly.

The faintest flutter stirred beneath her palm—soft, like the brushing wings of a moth. A reminder, she wasn't alone. Not really. Life was still moving, quietly, steadily, deep inside her.

She smiled, just a little.

Then she made her way to the large sliding barn door, one hand on the iron handle, ready to shut it for the day.

That's when her phone rang.

She fished it from her jacket pocket. "Beechland Equine Rescue, Virginia speaking," she answered, slipping easily into her new name—*her real* name now.

There was a pause, then: "Hi, Jen—sorry, Virginia. It's Mary. I've got a tough one for you… if you're ready."

Jenny stood still, the door half-closed behind her, the phone warm against her cheek. Outside, the wind moved through the trees like a whisper. Inside, the barn waited.

Then, from behind her, familiar arms wrapped around her waist. A strong, steady presence. Tristan pressed a kiss to the back of her neck, his breath warm against her skin. He said nothing, just held her there.

Jenny closed her eyes.

"I'm ready," she said.

"***We're*** ready," Tristan whispered.

"We're ready," Virginia said to Mary.

And they were. They really were…

~ The End ~

www.ingramcontent.com/pod-product-compliance
Lightning Source LLC
Chambersburg PA
CBHW070317260626
47160CB00003B/874